My Mother's Secret

My Mother's Secret

Based on a True Holocaust Story

J. L. Witterick

PENGUIN
an imprint of Penguin Canada Books Inc.

Published by the Penguin Group
Penguin Canada Books Inc.,
90 Eglinton Avenue East, Suite 700, Toronto, Ontario, Canada M4P 2Y3

Penguin Group (USA) Inc., 375 Hudson Street, New York, New York 10014, U.S.A.
Penguin Books Ltd, 80 Strand, London WC2R 0RL, England
Penguin Ireland, 25 St Stephen's Green, Dublin 2, Ireland (a division of Penguin Books Ltd)
Penguin Group (Australia), 707 Collins Street, Melbourne, Victoria 3008, Australia
(a division of Pearson Australia Group Pty Ltd)
Penguin Books India Pvt Ltd, 11 Community Centre, Panchsheel Park,
New Delhi – 110 017, India
Penguin Group (NZ), 67 Apollo Drive, Rosedale, Auckland 0632, New Zealand
(a division of Pearson New Zealand Ltd)
Penguin Books (South Africa) (Pty) Ltd, 24 Sturdee Avenue, Rosebank,
Johannesburg 2196, South Africa

Penguin Books Ltd, Registered Offices: 80 Strand, London WC2R 0RL, England

Published in Penguin hardcover by Penguin Canada Books Inc., 2013
Simultaneously published in the United States by G.P. Putnam's Sons

2 3 4 5 6 7 8 9 10

Book design by Gretchen Achilles

Manufactured in the U.S.A.

ISBN: 978-0-670-06810-4

American Library of Congress Cataloging in Publication data available

Visit the Penguin Canada website at **www.penguin.ca**

Special and corporate bulk purchase rates available; please see
www.penguin.ca/corporatesales or call 1-800-810-3104, ext. 2477.

Dedicated to Jim Hunter . . . the bravest man I know,

and to those who risked their lives to save others

known as the Righteous among the Nations

Praise for *My Mother's Secret*

"A poignant reminder of what can happen, and a tale of incredible courage."

—TONY GAGE, *Board of Governors, University of Victoria*

"My granddaughter says it's the best book she's ever read!"

—HAROLD J. WOLFE, *Board of Trustees, the Jewish Theological Seminary; Chairman, Beth Tzedec Foundation of Toronto*

"I have always had an acute interest in history as it relates to the Holocaust. *My Mother's Secret* took my breath away!"

—BRIAN GOLDSTEIN, *President, CCMH*

"A touching, humane work that celebrates the power of love, the attributes of leadership, and the importance of family."

—MARGARET SOUTHERN, *Companion of the Order of Canada, Lieutenant of the Royal Victorian Order, Alberta Order of Excellence*

"It is a luxury to be able to read lots and lots of books; most are enjoyable, but some make you stop and think. This book is one of those—it has a Jonathan Livingston Seagull quality to it."

—RICHARD S. SELF, *Head, Marketing and Communications, RBC Global Asset Management*

"The story will take you on a heartfelt journey. The writing is exquisite ... simple, yet profound."

—MARY THROOP, *President, Summerhill Capital Management*

"I was very moved from start to finish by both the evocative content and the simple yet spellbinding manner in which the story unfolded."

—ELI RUBENSTEIN, *National Director, March of the Living Canada*

"An inspiring story that deals with choices, courage, and life's meaning."

—Kim Shannon, *President and CIO, Sionna Investment Managers*

"Unbelievable! What an amazing read! I LOVED this story."

—Ted Manziaris, *President and Cofounder, Turtle Island Recycling Corporation*

"True heroism is when no one sees or knows. A truly inspiring and breathtaking book."

—Rabbi Chaim Boyarsky

"*My Mother's Secret* is excellent! The strong message is told in a quiet and unforgettable way."

—Pam Mountain, *Branch Head, Annette Street Library*

"I was taken by the story. It is beautifully written, moving, and lovely."

—Trevor Dighton, *former CFO and Executive Director, G4S*

"This is a captivating story of amazing courage and heroism."

—Dr. Patrick Gullane, CM, MB, FRCSC, *Order of Canada*

"*My Mother's Secret* is a compelling read!"

—Dr. Susan R. Groesbeck, *Principal, Havergal College*

"I really loved the whole book. Every sentence was enthralling. It was a perfect balance of danger, romance, and history."

—Alexandra Philp, *13*

"From the moment I started to read *My Mother's Secret*, I couldn't put it down. It captivated me. I just loved it!"

—Barb Simpson, *Vice President, International Banking, Scotiabank*

"I can see this novel changing and touching many hearts ... including mine."

—Anita Pyclik, *Literature and History Major*

The book was inspired by the courage of Franciszka Halamajowa and her daughter, Helena. The characters are fictional. Nevertheless, many of the experiences of the characters are consistent with events of that time.

To remain silent and indifferent is the greatest sin of all.

—Elie Wiesel

Part I

HELENA

Chapter 1

When you're a child, you think that your parents are the same as everyone else's and that what happens in your house happens in other people's homes too. You have no way of knowing any differently.

And so, I think that everyone is afraid of their father. I think that men marry to have someone cook and clean for them. I don't know that some men actually love their wives and their children.

My brother, Damian, and I grow up with two very different people.

My father is precise, hard, and linear, while my mother is imaginative, loving, and warm.

Both are strong.

My father is Ukrainian and my mother is Polish, but we

moved to Germany, where the opportunities are better than in Poland.

My father is a machinist, and that suits him well because it requires precision and measurement—both skills he possesses in abundance.

My mother works as a cook for a wealthy German family, and we love that she often brings leftovers home for us. She brings food that we never would have tasted otherwise. Not much usually, but there are sometimes small pieces of expensive meats like pork chops and, if we're lucky, fruits and nuts, which are luxuries for most people.

When there are leftovers, my mother puts them all on a plate for us to share. Even though we would have already eaten the dinner cooked ahead for us in the morning, it's a special treat that we all look forward to. Typically, my father gorges himself, reaching for more even while he's still chewing with his mouth partly open.

Once as I am about to pick up a slice of apple from the plate, my father slaps my hand. It is something that he wants.

My mother sees this and shakes her head. The next week she keeps a whole apple in her pocket and only brings it out after my father starts the loud, snorting sound that is his snore when asleep.

She cuts the apple in half and gives it to my brother and me.

I don't know why, but I remember what happens next more than I remember how my father treats me. I can hear the words from my brother as if he has just said them: "Lena," he says, using his nickname for me, "you know I ate so much for dinner that I really don't want anything else. Why don't you have my half too?"

I shake my head. "You can eat this, Damian." But he refuses and makes me take it.

It makes the apple even sweeter than it already is.

My father, not having seen a trace of an apple for some time, asks, "Why aren't you bringing home any apples, Franciszka?"

My mother shrugs her shoulders and says, "I work there; I don't shop there. I can only bring home what they give me."

My brother and I look at each other and then down because, if we didn't, he would have seen our smiles.

Two strong people living together is not easy to begin with, but two strong people with opposing political views—that's virtually impossible.

My father is a Nazi sympathizer, and my mother is horrified by it.

"Hitler is the answer to the problems of the German people," my father says.

Just a few years ago no one had even heard of Hitler, but now it seems like his name is everywhere. His wave of popularity is swelling. People are poor and unemployment is high. Hitler promises better times. He tells the German people that they are superior.

"Germany will be a great power again if Hitler is the leader," my father says. His fellow workers at the machine shop are all going to vote for him.

"If you're German and someone tells you that you're born superior, that would sound pretty good," my mother says.

"Even better if the bad times are not your fault but caused by the Jewish people. It's so much easier than trying to explain it logically."

My mother doesn't pass judgment on groups of people. She believes in the individual.

"Not all Germans are good or bad, and the same with Jews," she says.

She's outspoken and says what she believes.

They have shouting matches over this, and while my brother and I stay quiet, we don't like what Hitler is promising. We heard Hitler speak once and saw the hypnotic power that he had over people.

He has that effect on our father.

My father doesn't argue with facts. He makes his points with attacks on the other person.

He doesn't fight fair.

"What do you know about politics?" he says to my mother. "Cooking makes you smart, does it?"

"It doesn't make you blind" is what she says.

I think to myself, *I will never marry anyone like my father.*

Chapter 2

I don't know if my mother ever loved my father.

Maybe love isn't something that people value when it's hard just to get by.

Damian and I are constantly worried that our father, so quick to anger, will strike her in one of their arguments.

Being slight and about half his size, my mother would be seriously injured.

She never backs down in their arguments, so it is my brother and I who fear.

We want to grow up so desperately.

Chapter 3

As predicted by my father, Hitler becomes chancellor on January 30, 1933.

Seven months later, a law is introduced to ban the formation of parties.

Now . . . there is no stopping the Nazi machine.

Chapter 4

It may have been as subtle as the sight of a small robin sitting on our windowsill in the early days of spring that makes my mother think, *This simple bird has the freedom to fly anywhere, and yet here we stay.*

Or maybe it's just what is practical. Leave when you have enough money set aside.

Regardless, one uneventful day, she tells my father that she has decided to move back to Poland. This is the same as saying she is leaving him because he has on many occasions said that he would never return to a country he felt was backward compared to Germany.

At this point, my brother is eighteen and I am two years younger, so we can make our own decision in terms of whom we will live with.

In reality, there's no decision to make.

We respect that she stands up to my father, who promises a secure lifestyle for obedience.

Sometimes I wonder if it's because we never felt close to our father that we embraced the values of our mother. It's hard to say how we become the people we do. My mother believes that it comes from our choices. She says, "If you choose to do the right thing, it's a conscious decision at first. Then it becomes second nature. You don't have to think about what is right because doing the right thing becomes who you are, like a reflex. Your actions with time become your character."

"If you leave, don't come back," are my father's last words to us.

Chapter 5

We don't take much when we leave.

Fortunately, my mother has been smart enough to keep some of her earnings hidden from my father.

With her savings, my mother buys a small house with some land for raising chickens and growing vegetables in her hometown of Sokal, Poland.

Sokal is located a day's wagon ride from Warsaw. There's a river with majestic willow trees lining the banks that runs through town. In the summer, it has a carefree feel to it.

The people living here form three distinct communities: Ukrainian, Polish, and Jewish.

The Ukrainians don't trust the Poles, the Poles don't trust the Ukrainians, and they both don't trust the Jews. There exists a certain friction that has been dulled by time but is never gone.

A few wealthy families live in Sokal, but most of the people are of modest means. Just about everyone works hard for what they have.

The more expensive homes in town are made from bricks. However, the majority of people live in homes made from wooden boards that are considerably cheaper. Fireplaces are used to keep warm in the winter, when it can be mercilessly cold. It's not unusual for people to wear almost as much to keep warm indoors as outdoors in the coldest months.

For water, people go to a well that's in their neighborhood. Farmers sell their produce and meats in the market, where most people shop. Only those with money shop in the stores, which carry imported goods from Germany and other places.

At the market, my mother sells eggs from our chickens, and garden vegetables that she grows in season. My brother works at an oil refinery a few towns away, so we only see him on his days off. He brings supplies and takes care of us more than my father ever did.

When my brother comes to visit, the first thing he does is pick me up and whirl me around as if I were a small child. I am dizzy with this but love the feeling. Over six feet in height, he towers above me. I have to look up at him because I am barely taller than my five-foot mother.

"I don't know how two plain-looking people like your

father and I could have produced such attractive children," my mother says.

It seems we did inherit the best features from both our parents.

I have my father's brown eyes and chestnut hair, which flows with a natural wave hinting at its origin from his tight curls. My brother has my mother's fair skin and light hair, and I am envious of their gray, sparkling eyes.

Damian always brings me an apple when he comes to visit.

It's love and sacrifice disguised as a piece of fruit.

He brings my mother chewing tobacco, which she adores.

On my seventeenth birthday, Damian surprises me with an apple tree. "Now you can have apples whenever you like, Lena. You don't have to wait for me anymore," he says. "Show me where you want it planted."

I choose a spot just outside my window. It will be the first thing I see when I wake up.

I can't wait until I can earn money too. I want to surprise him with a present, and I already have something in mind.

There is a beautiful brown leather jacket in a store on the way to the market, which would be perfect for Damian.

I keep thinking to myself, *Please, please don't let anyone else buy it before I can get the money.*

Chapter 6

In the local newspaper, there's an ad for a secretarial position, assisting the general manager of a garment factory in town. I confide to my mother that even though my chances are slim, I want to try. "There are going to be so many girls competing for this job," I say.

She says to me, "Do you remember when you first learned how to type? You wanted to be faster than anyone else in your class, but we didn't have a typewriter so you drew the keyboard on a piece of paper and practiced as if you were really typing. You always wanted to be the best, Helena, and you practiced day and night. Your teacher told me that she never had a student who could type eighty words a minute. You were the top in your class then, so why shouldn't you be selected for this job now? Besides, how many girls speak German as beautifully as you?"

I already knew everything she was telling me, but there are times when it feels good to hear what you already know.

My mother somehow manages to provide me with the most beautiful dress I have ever seen for the interview. It's made from soft wool, a fabric that only wealthy people can afford. The cream color is professional, yet fresh and classic. The dress is fitted from the waist upward with three-quarter sleeves and a V-neck. At the waist, it flares out to a full skirt, flattering my figure. Around my neck I wear a simple pearl strand, which is the only jewelry that my mother owns. My shoes are old, but I shine them up with some polish. This dress transforms me and gives me the confidence to compete against girls who I know will be better educated and from far more prestigious families.

Before I leave, my mother says to me, "They would be smart to hire you. You're capable, honest, and hardworking. When you smile, Helena, your face lights up and there is nothing more beautiful, so if it is a man interviewing you, smile." That's my mother—always knowing what to say and providing insightful advice as well.

MR. KOWALSKI, a man in his late twenties, is younger and more handsome than I expect. With him is Ferda, an older, heavyset woman who is also part of the interview. He tests me with conversation in German and asks me to type a short letter, which he dictates rather quickly in Polish.

I know my German is good, and I type faster than anyone I know, so I'm scoring well on both accounts. His final question is, "Helena, if you could choose one thing to possess, what would it be: breathtaking beauty, worldly knowledge, or financial wealth?"

With this question, he's trying to figure out what kind of person I am. It's important to answer correctly, but I say what makes the most sense to me. "I would take the money."

He looks surprised, while Ferda looks openly disgusted at my crass response. This is neither the answer they expected nor the answer they have heard from the other candidates.

He clears his throat a bit. "You would take the money? Why?"

"Well, being beautiful doesn't last. Having worldly knowledge is good, but money feeds hungry stomachs. Also, if I had money, I could study what I want and learn all sorts of things. I could afford books and teachers. Money gives you choices. It gives you freedom and the ability to look after other people. Yes, I'll take the money."

I hear my own voice, and it sounds much more confident than I really am.

Mr. Kowalski now has an amused look on his face. It's not what he expected.

He says, "Thank you very much. We will make our decision shortly and get back to you."

Before I turn to leave, I look directly at him and smile.

I get the job.

Chapter 7

The apple tree in bloom is full of white flowers that fill the air with beauty and sweetness. When there is a breeze, the fragrance sweeps through my window. On these mornings, it feels like only good things can happen.

I don't know how it started, maybe it was the smile, but Mr. Kowalski clearly prefers my company over that of Ferda, who is the office manager. When there are project deadlines, he asks me to work late with him. He is always a gentleman, and I don't feel uncomfortable in any way.

One evening, he asks if I would like to have dinner with him since we were both working so late. I reply that I would be very pleased to, which is the truth. Over a simple dinner in the neighborhood restaurant, we take a break from talking about the company business and begin to know each other as two people sharing a meal might do.

He is the son of a wealthy industrialist in Germany who owns the factory. His Polish mother was his father's mistress. Although he admires his father, he resents that he and his mother lived in the shadow of his father's legitimate family.

I know that he is well educated, so his father must have paid for that. He also has the factory's top job, which most men his age would just be working their way up to.

I see that he knows that he is where he is because of his father, and there's a vulnerability to him because of it.

I say to him, "You may have obtained the job because of your father, but you do a good job because of who you are."

I think he appreciated that.

Funny how even the most successful people still need re-assurance, wherever it may come from.

I also tell him that not having to share a father doesn't necessarily mean that you have a better relationship. "We haven't heard from my father since we left Germany," I say, carefully omitting the fact that my father is a Nazi sympathizer.

Now that I know Casmir better, I feel safe enough to ask something that has been on my mind since the interview. "Why did you choose me? There were so many others."

"Well, if it was up to Ferda, we wouldn't be sitting here right now," he says with a mischievous smile that makes him look boyish.

"You were brave enough to tell me the truth, and I want someone I can trust. Honesty is refreshing, Helena. Besides, you have that great smile and type like lightning."

He is laughing as he finishes saying this, and I start laughing too.

Was it because he trusted me enough to reveal his darkness, or was it that I had not expected to be in the company of a man so different from the harshness of my own father, that I begin to have feelings yet unknown to me?

Despite our different worlds, we feel closer after that night.

Chapter 8

I find that I now fuss about my appearance before leaving for work. I wake up earlier to make sure that my hair is in the right place. I spend a little money for lipstick, and I ask my mother if she can find any more of those beautiful dresses.

I look forward to work and am excited when I see Casmir. At the office, we address each other politely as Mr. Kowalski and Miss Halamajowa. However, over dinner, which is now at least once a week, we call each other by our first names, Casmir and Helena.

I can't remember when the presents started. It's usually when he returns from a trip to Germany. There are chocolates, books, and scarves—nothing too grand to imply seriousness, but always something to let me know that he thought of me.

Not having much to give in return, I occasionally bring him a home-cooked German dish that my mother has made.

"Helena, how does your mother know my favorite foods? Maybe I should be bringing her presents too," he says playfully. Casmir enjoys those meals immensely.

I AM SO HAPPY, and it is an odd time to be happy.

The world is in turmoil.

There is news that the Nazis will soon be in Poland, and while we know it, there is not much that we can do.

Everyone is nervous.

Casmir is probably the only person I know who is calm about this development. His friends include Germans and high-ranking officials.

Chapter 9

Germany invades Poland on September 1, 1939, and it takes them just over a month to conquer the country. The ineffectiveness of Poland's defenses leaves the population deflated.

I don't understand much about the war, and especially why Hitler decided to invade Poland, so I ask Casmir, who seems to know all these things.

"Hitler invaded Poland because he thought that Britain and France would let him get away with it."

I say, "What do you mean?"

Casmir makes it simple for me: "Well, he didn't think that they would declare war over it.

"You see, most people have until now thought that communism was a bigger threat than Hitler. For that reason, they let Germany rearm over the past few years, even though it was against the treaty for Germany to do so after the last war. They thought that a strong Germany would be a good balance to Russia.

"Think about it; didn't Germany host the Olympics just three years ago?

"The world wants to think he's a good guy.

"Hitler is counting on this.

"What did the British do while German soldiers were crossing into Poland? Despite declaring their support for Poland, the might of the Royal Air Force consisted of dropping leaflets asking Germany to reconsider their attack."

Casmir lowers his voice. "They should have been dropping bombs if they were serious."

I realize then that Poland didn't have the support of the friends that we thought. How could the world have been so misled?

Casmir continues. "Britain and France came through after the invasion and declared war on Germany, so Hitler miscalculated their response. But he's made an alliance with Stalin to strengthen his position, and they have agreed to split Poland between them."

This explains why our town has Germans on one side of the river and Russians on the other.

We're on the Russian side.

Chapter 10

When the Russians first arrive, they want to assimilate their communist culture and begin arresting Polish officers, intellectuals, large-estate owners, and former civil servants.

The Polish community is shaken, as anyone deemed a threat to communist thinking is either executed or sent to labor camps.

Neighbors turn on one another.

Anyone with a grudge can make an accusation that will result in an arrest.

No one feels safe under these circumstances, and the tension is high.

Being unimportant and poor turns out to be a good thing, as my mother and I are left alone.

Damian is considered an essential laborer, so he is safe as well.

Casmir is well connected and untouchable in a different way.

This is a world where to be insignificant, necessary, or connected is the best way to survive.

Chapter 11

War gives you a sense of urgency about your life because there is so much death waiting for a chance. Maybe that's why it's possible to feel love in the midst of so much chaos.

One day Ferda and I are alone in the lunchroom, and she says to me, "Who do you think you are?"

"What do you mean, Ferda?" I ask innocently, even though I suspect she means my relationship with Casmir.

She says, "You're a peasant girl with no father and no money. Do you really think you're suitable for Mr. Kowalski?"

I say, "We have a very professional relationship but happen to enjoy each other's company."

She says, "I never liked you, but I'm going to do you a favor and tell you a secret. Mr. Kowalski is engaged to a girl in Germany, and that's why he's always going there. His father knows the girl's family, and, unlike you, she's well educated and comes from a respectable German family."

I feel sick.

I don't know where I had thought my relationship with Casmir would eventually lead, but this news shatters me. Casmir going to Germany to be with his fiancée? Were my gifts leftovers from what he had bought her?

He doesn't owe me anything and I know that, but I can't help feeling overwhelmed by this news. I keep my composure with Ferda and then excuse myself after lunch. I go to the bathroom and throw up what little I have managed to swallow. For the rest of the day, I try to focus on my work but am mindless in my motions.

I am lying in bed, hugging my pillow and crying, when my mother finds me.

She sits next to me and softly caresses my hair. "What's wrong, Helena?"

I shake my head. How do you tell your mother that if you weren't her daughter but that of some wealthy family, it would solve the problem? No, that isn't it. I feel sad and hollow and can't explain my feelings.

My mother doesn't press further. She just sits with me until I fall asleep.

Later that night, I tell her that Casmir is engaged to a girl in Germany.

She says, "How do you know?"

"Ferda told me," I answer.

"Is Ferda your friend?"

She knows the answer to this question from what I have told her before, but she wants me to come to my own conclusion.

"Do you trust Casmir?" she asks.

"Yes," I say, and I do.

"Well then, why don't you ask him yourself and see what he says?" my mother suggests.

"I'm too embarrassed," I say sheepishly.

"Do you want to know the truth?" She pursues this further. "I thought you told me that what you liked most about him was that you could talk about anything."

She is right.

I need to speak to him.

Casmir is away in Germany and will be coming back later in the week. We had planned to have dinner at the restaurant that has become our regular place.

I decide that will be a good time to be up-front about the situation.

Right away when Casmir sees me, he knows something's off.

That happens when you're close to someone.

He waits until we're at the restaurant to ask me what is on my mind.

I choose my words and speak slowly. "Ferda tells me that you're engaged to a girl in Germany. It surprised me." I can't look at him when I say this.

He has been watching me seriously, but then quite unexpectedly he changes his expression completely and lets out a chuckle. Quickly he adds, "I am not making light of this, Helena. It's just funny that Ferda knows that I'm engaged before I do. Is there a date for the wedding too?"

I look at his boyish grin and then burst out laughing. It feels like old times.

Casmir explains that his father wanted him to meet the daughter of a good friend of his, and so he did. But he had no intention of pursuing it further than that.

"She's not as pretty or as smart as you, Helena." How does he know exactly what to say? Am I that transparent? Regardless, transparent or not, I am too happy to care.

THE NEXT DAY, Ferda is fired.

I didn't know Casmir was that angry.

Chapter 12

In June 1941, Hitler breaks his pact with Stalin and the Germans move to our side of the river. It seems like we have gone from bad to worse. The Nazis start persecuting the Jews just as the Russians did to the Poles, but they don't discriminate. They treat all Jews, rich and poor, equally badly.

We notice how the Germans start by denying Jews their ability to work and shop. It then moves to their loss of freedom, when all the Jews in town are imprisoned in the ghetto.

At random, Jews are selected to be executed, and this creates terror among their population.

I wish I could wipe out the images of children crying as they are pulled from their fathers' arms, of old men struggling as they are made to dance with shots fired at their feet, of soldiers laughing as they take what they want from stores without paying.

I don't want to see the cruelty of men, but it is impossible not to witness such brutal acts on a daily basis.

How can people do this to each other?

Chapter 13

Casmir is the light that brightens my world, which is becoming darker by the day.

If he is ever afraid, no one would know.

People gravitate to him, to his charm and his lightness, so rare in these times.

Casmir finds out that the local German commander is recently married and has a wife in Germany. Cleverly, he arranges for a car to pick her up and drive her to Sokal for a visit. Casmir's father owns the hotel in town. In her room, there are flowers, chocolates, and wine to make sure she is happy when she sees her husband.

The commander is elated to see his wife and ever so grateful to Casmir.

From there, it is effortless for Casmir to become good friends with the man who is the most feared in Sokal.

Chapter 14

It has been four years since I have been seeing Casmir, but it feels like I have known him all my life. He has a way of making me feel safe and happy—something I have never known before.

When I am with him, everything else fades away. The world is a good place, and there is no war to think about. There is nothing except the face of the man I love.

One day, we are at our regular restaurant and have just finished dinner when he says, "My father is ill, Helena. He needs me in Germany. I have to move back."

Every part of my body is shouting, "No, don't go!" but I sit there in silence.

I start crying, and I hate that.

He says, "Come with me, Helena."

He thinks that should make me stop crying, but now I really lose control.

I'm not pretty when I cry this hard, because my face gets all squished up. My nose is red and my eyes swell up, but I can't help any of it.

I want to go with him more than anything, but I can't.

I can't stop crying because there's so much to say and none of it can be said.

In our small house and shed, my mother and I are hiding two Jewish families!

She needs me to help buy the food, so it isn't obvious that we are feeding many people. I can't imagine leaving her with such a large responsibility.

At times I resent that she has hidden these families. There are nights when I wake up sweating with nightmares of German soldiers breaking down our door. I cannot be truthful with Casmir, and that is very hard.

Whenever I feel this way, I think of the day we heard it—unbelievable sounds from the ghetto where they were keeping all the Jews from Sokal. There were gunshots, screaming, and explosions.

It makes me shiver. I know why we had to do what we did, but that didn't make it any easier.

I dare not tell Casmir about my internal conflicts.

I say, "I love you more than anything, and I would go if I could."

"I don't understand," he says.

I say, "I can't leave my mother."

He replies with relief. "Is that all? My father has a big apartment for me, and she can have her own room with us."

Not workable, I think, and I scramble to make something up. "She feels safe in that house and doesn't want to leave."

The thing with a lie is that soon more become necessary to cover up the ones before it. And so I continue with, "After my brother is married, she will live with him."

It's hard to think clearly when you're this upset, so I don't even know if anything I am saying makes sense.

In any case, Casmir is just as upset as I am, so he doesn't question it.

"When do you have to leave?" I ask.

"By the end of the month," he replies.

"So soon?" It was the response that I would have had, no matter what the answer was.

He says, "I will come back to see you when I can."

All of a sudden, the realization of what I've done hits me.

I feel myself panicking.

I want to say, "Take me with you, forget what I've just said," but I know I can't. The thought of being away from him is unbearable and I start to sob uncontrollably.

What he says next catches me completely by surprise. "Helena, let's get engaged."

Did he plan on asking me all along, or is he reacting to the distraught girl in front of him?

"Really?" I say, my voice cracking as I try to suppress a sniffle.

"Really is not an answer," he says.

Even now, he is the Casmir that makes everything better.

"What will your father say?" I ask timidly.

"It doesn't matter," he says in a dismissive manner. "He's old and tired now. He won't make me repeat his mistake."

"What mistake?" I ask.

Casmir says, "I never told you that my mother committed suicide, Helena."

I am taken aback by this.

"When his wife found out about my mother, she threatened to divorce him if he kept seeing her.

"So he told my mother that he had to end the relationship. After she died, he never forgave himself. In a letter she left for him, she made him promise to take care of me and told him that she would always love him. It was then that I was sent to a boarding school in Switzerland."

"Oh, Casmir," I say, and now the tears are for him. "It must have been horrible for you."

He says, "I didn't know how to think of my father for the longest time. He loved me but kept me distant from his family. He visited me at school, but I never went home on holidays like the other boys. Now that he thinks his time may be limited, he wants me near him. When I see him, all he wants to talk about is my mother. He tells me that she was the one who really loved him. My father doesn't care that his wife hears him when he says, 'Not like this one. All she wants is the money.'"

Casmir tells me that his father wants him to have his business in Germany.

I didn't know that Casmir had suffered such loss as a child. He hid it well.

I need to make him understand even more than ever now.

I say, "Please wait for me, Casmir. I know how much your mother must have loved your father because that is how I feel about you."

We leave the restaurant, and he walks me home with his arm over my shoulder. I love that feeling.

Casmir hires someone to replace him at work, but everyone knows that we are engaged so I am treated very well.

Sometimes I think of Ferda and what she would think of this.

Almost every day, I wish for the war to be over.

Chapter 15

One day, my mother says, "Casmir is good friends with the German commander, right?"

I reply, "Yes, I told you this."

She says, "Well, then, let's invite them both over for dinner before he leaves."

I look at my mother as if she has lost her mind. I don't have to say that we have a Jewish family underneath the table where we are sitting and another one in the shed.

She says, "Wouldn't it be a great idea to let our neighbors think that we have friends in high places?"

I am educated, but my mother is smarter.

So I invite Casmir and his friend over for a home-cooked German dinner.

The neighbors look out their windows and doors as the

black, polished car carrying the commander and two guards arrive at our house.

There will be lots of gossip tonight.

Our neighbors think that my mother is a *Volksdeutsche*, which is an ethnic German, and so she is regarded as someone of higher status. She isn't but acts as if she is.

We buy more food than we need, but who would know that some of that food is intended to feed the families we are hiding? We have sausages, sauerkraut, potatoes, cake, and beer. Casmir has slipped me extra money to make it a special meal.

Incredibly, everyone has a wonderful time, and I temporarily forget that we are putting our lives in harm's way.

Could these possibly be the same soldiers who were shooting the people in the ghetto? It seems unreal.

After that night and even with Casmir gone, we make dinner with the commander a regular event. My mother is a very good cook, and in the warmth of our small home, the war is far away for everyone who is tired of it.

We don't have many friends because it's too dangerous.

Seen to be friends with the Nazis, people with whom we would want to be friends don't want to be friends with us. And people who want to be our friends, we don't want.

Chapter 16

Casmir has been away for two weeks and still no word.

I am worried about him and ask my mother as soon as I come home from work every day if there is any news.

She says, "Don't worry, Helena. Casmir is smart. Nothing will happen to him. It just takes longer for mail to be delivered with the war."

Then one day, I arrive home to find a big package on the kitchen table.

"For you, Helena," my mother says with a smile.

It is from Casmir.

I cut the strings and pull the brown paper apart with great excitement.

There is a beautiful, warm coat for me and hidden inside the pockets are chocolates, nylons, soap, and a letter.

"Look, Mama," I say. "Isn't he wonderful?"

She nods as I fly past her with the letter held to my chest. I want to read it in the privacy of the bedroom.

Dear Helena,

Are you well?

I didn't think I could miss anyone so much.

Not a moment goes by when my mind doesn't wander back to you.

I'll be getting dressed or even talking to someone, and there you are.

The other day, I had a piece of apple strudel and it reminded me of the story you told me about your brother.

Everything reminds me of you.

I've never felt this way before.

My father's health is poor, but he is not dying as he led me to believe.

I think he just wanted to make sure I would come.

I am very busy, as he has transferred his factories in Germany over to me, and I am running all three of them. He says his two daughters have never shown an interest in the business, so he is leaving them with apartment buildings, which will provide rental income.

You should have heard how furious his wife was when she found out. He says to me, "You must stay or she will find a way to get the factories when I die. She's all about the money, even though she will have the hotels and the house."

My father can't complain enough about his wife. He has a picture of my mother beside his bed, and I'm sure it's not appreciated by his wife.

Although I have no feelings for this woman, I do know that she has no chance competing with the photo of my mother, captured in the prime of her beauty and glowing with love for the father of her child.

We're lucky, Helena, because we love each other for who we are. Do you know how rare that is? To find someone you love above all else and who in turn loves you the same way? What is that—one in a million?

I will come to visit in a few weeks. I have told my father that I need to check on the factory.

I can't wait to see you.

Yours most truly,
Casmir

I can hear his voice in the words.

Lying on my bed, I read the letter over and over again. Hugging the message that is him, I close my eyes to feel his presence. I see his face, the face that transforms the world for me.

I miss him so much. It's like being hungry all the time but worse because there's no cure without him.

I find some paper and write back.

Dear Casmir,

I was so happy to receive your letter and am very excited that you can come for a visit.

Thank you for sending me such a beautiful coat. When I wear it, it will feel like you are wrapped all around me, and I will be warm just from the thought of it.

You are right—we are very lucky to have found each other.

I never knew what it was like to feel this way about someone.

I am happiest when I am with you.

Even though we are apart, you should know that I am always with you.

I can't wait to see you and am counting the days until you return.

With great affection,

Helena

I didn't have anything to send him, so I picked a blossom from my tree and tucked it in the folded letter.

THE WORDS I wrote were meant to make him feel loved.

The letter I could never write tells him about how shaken I am after seeing a woman shot on the street, or how terrified I am of buying so much food, or how exhausted I am of constantly pretending to be friends with the Germans.

I want to tell Casmir all these things and more. I long for him to tell me that everything will be all right—even if no one can.

Chapter 17

Unknown to me, Vilheim, one of the commander's guards, has been visiting my mother while I am at work.

One evening, my mother whispers to me, "Vilheim is hiding with us."

She explains that they were going to send him to Russia. "He begged me to hide him," she says.

I look at my mother. I don't risk words, but with my hands I ask where. Where could we possibly hide him in this small house?

My mother points to the attic.

I whisper, "Is he there now?"

My mother nods.

I know the attic is impossibly small, and I remember that Vilheim is quite tall, so he must have to lie perfectly flat to fit.

My mother continues in a low voice. "He's going to come down for a quick stretch at night, so I thought you should know and not be surprised."

Over the next few days, my mother tells me more about Vilheim. "He is an only child and was raised by his grandmother in Germany. He grew up on a farm and loves animals. He's about the same age as Damian. He's really sweet, Helena, not like the other soldiers."

I think only my mother could use the word *sweet* to describe a German soldier in the middle of a war.

The first time I see Vilheim come down, it is late at night. He's a bit awkward with me, but he smiles shyly and says, "Thank you," with a kind of humble appreciation. Then quickly he goes back to the attic, where I know it must feel like a prison.

I see why my mother agreed to help him. This boy couldn't hurt anyone.

We develop a code to let Vilheim know when it is safe to come down. My mother takes our broom and taps the ceiling three times.

We are hiding both Jews and Germans.

I wish that I could tell Casmir, but this is the one thing that I absolutely cannot reveal.

My mother says, "It's better that Casmir doesn't know because then he can be truthful if we are caught."

The thought makes me shudder.

ONE OF OUR NEIGHBORS notices that my mother visits the well frequently and asks why she needs so much water.

She says, "I have a skin disease and need to bathe frequently."

"Can you imagine?" my mother says to me later. "We're in the middle of a war and someone has the time to wonder about why I am using so much water!"

If a neighbor notices such a small thing like this, I can't help but wonder if Casmir suspects anything.

Chapter 18

I long to be with Casmir and feel frustrated at being caught between what is right and what I want.

My mother senses this and doesn't scold me for my short temper and moodiness.

Instead, she tells me a story about myself.

She says, "When you were about eight years old, you found a cat that was injured and lying on the side of the road. Its leg was badly damaged and covered in blood. It looked like it was going to die, if it wasn't dead already. You picked it up and brought it home. I helped you clean the leg, and we kept the cat warm and fed it leftovers. When it recovered, we let it go. Sometimes it would come back for a visit, and we both knew that it remembered us.

"Helena, there are three kinds of people in the world. One that would have seen the suffering cat and not have given it a second thought. Another that would have seen the same cat and said to themselves, 'Oh, isn't that a pity,' before continuing about their business. Finally, there is the kind who sees the suffering, feels the empathy, and then goes one step further by taking action to help. That is you. You didn't leave the cat there to perish. I am proud that you are my daughter. Think what a wonderful place the world would be if everyone was like that."

I know what she is really saying.

I had agreed to hide the Jewish families. It's just that I miss Casmir so much.

Chapter 19

Damian has done quite well and is promoted to manager at the oil refinery.

It makes me so happy to see him wearing the leather jacket that I bought with my first paycheck.

Every four weeks he comes with kerosene, machine oil, olive oil, and cottonseed oil for my mother to trade for food with the other peasants. One time, he even has his workers bring a wagon full of firewood to make sure we can stay warm through the winter.

We don't see much of my brother because on his days off work, he is secretly transporting supplies to the partisan Jews hiding in the forest.

On a cold, bleak evening, a man we have never seen before appears at our house. He says that he is in the underground with Damian. He looks weary and worn when he says to my mother, "I am very sorry to tell you that your son, Damian, was killed today. His wagon was ambushed. It's risky for me to come here, but I thought it was important for you to know that he was a hero."

Shortly after telling us this, he leaves.

My mother is a strong woman in every way, but she is broken inside with this. Do we really heal stronger where we are broken? I don't think so because it feels like neither one of us will recover, ever.

I so desperately want to see my brother again.

I go outside and sit under the apple tree.

Wrapping my arms around my knees, I bury my head in my lap.

I see my ten-year-old brother. We have just finished dinner, my father, brother, and I. My mother eats later when she comes home. My brother is clearing the table, while my father is dozing in his chair in the living room. I am washing my father's favorite ceramic beer stein, when it slips from my hand. I watch in horror as it drops to the floor. I am frozen with fear. My father rushes over with the crashing sound and my brother is fast to respond with "I dropped it, Papa. I didn't mean to. It was an accident."

"You stupid, useless idiot. Do you know how much that cost?" My father takes off his leather belt and starts to whip my brother, who is hunched over trying his best to protect his face.

I scream hysterically, "No, Papa! No! Stop hurting him. It was me! It was me! I dropped it."

My father stops whipping my brother and looks at me like a madman.

"So you're a liar too, are you?" He is fuming and pulls me over by my long hair.

His other hand is up with the belt ready to descend.

Without hesitation, my brother wraps his body around mine and shields me from what is coming.

I am crying and struggling to break free, but my brother is holding me too tightly.

I feel his pain worse than if it were my own.

I am screaming so loudly that we don't hear the door open until we see my mother pushing my father away. "Are you crazy, Borys? That's enough!"

He backs down, but not before saying, "Look at the mess your children made," pointing to the pieces on the floor.

She looks at us and signals with a tilt of her head for us to leave the room.

"Yes, I see," she says wearily. "I'll pick up another one for you tomorrow, all right?"

Either he's tired out by the whipping or is happy that he's

getting a new stein. Regardless, my father walks away grumbling about how useless we are.

Was Damian protecting someone else when he was killed? I can picture how he would defend his supplies, the lifeline of the Jews hiding in the forest.

I can't believe that I will never see him again or hear the special way he says, "Lena."

It feels like the sorrow is in my bones.

EVEN WITH OUR GRIEF, we have to be careful about how we tell people about Damian's death.

Our story to the neighbors is that he was killed in a robbery.

Casmir makes the trip from Germany and comes to the house when he hears.

He holds me and doesn't say much. Some things are beyond words.

Part II

Bronek

Chapter 20

My brother and I have been inseparable from as early as I can remember.

Although just a year younger, Dawid only comes up to my shoulder.

I have protected him all my life.

My mother says, "If you didn't both come out of my own body, I wouldn't have believed it."

One day, Dawid comes home from school with a bloody nose.

"What happened?" I ask, outraged that anyone would hurt him.

He says, "It was Resnit. He makes the kids give him a zloty every day or he beats them. I told him that I didn't have any money, but he didn't believe me."

I am furious.

I say to my brother, "You won't have to worry about Resnit after I deal with him tomorrow."

Dawid says, "I'm okay now, Bronek. Let's just forget about it."

My brother avoids confrontation. He's a peacemaker.

Not me.

The next day I go to school with Dawid and make him point out the bully to me.

I walk over to Resnit and, without a word, punch him hard in the face, breaking his nose. Then I follow with another blow to the stomach, so now he's fallen over.

In a cold voice I say, "If you ever touch my brother again, I'll kill you."

We live in Sokal, a small town on the banks of the Bug River in Poland. Word travels fast in a small place, and Dawid never has to worry about walking home from school after that.

Chapter 21

I should be in school myself, but I prefer to go to work with my father. I think secretly, he's happy that I want to be with him.

Books don't make much sense to me, as they do to Dawid.

My father, a strong man, teaches me to be handy with a hammer and takes me to construction jobs with him. His men respect that he always does more than his share. He covers for members of his team who are ill and can't do their job to justify the day's pay. You don't see men like my father every day, and I'm proud to be his son.

Walking home from our jobs, my father shares his dreams with me. "Bronek, one day you and I will build our own house. We'll use it to show people what we can do. If people see that a good house can be built for a reasonable price, then we'll have lots of business and make lots of money—maybe enough to buy your mother a fur coat," he says with a wink of his eye. "We'll be partners and we'll bring Dawid in too. With all his education, he can figure out how much money we'll be making, because we won't be able to count that high!"

I love that thought.

At home, my mother has a hot dinner ready and after the physical work all day, we can eat plenty. It's my favorite time of the day, partly because I love to eat but mostly because I love how we are all together.

Dawid always wants to hear about what we did. I know that my father is proud of me because he usually says, "Bronek is as good as any man that I have ever worked with." Then my mother typically says, "I am proud of both my boys." It happens like that almost every time, and yet I never tire of hearing it.

Every man has his weakness, and my father loves his drink. It's only occasionally that he loses control over the bottle, but it does happen. When he's drunk, he's just silly, not mean. My mother scolds him but never in a harsh way. It's hard to be angry with a good-natured giant like my father.

Not all fathers die because of the one flaw that they possess, but mine does.

One day after having too much to drink the night before,

my father falls off the roof of a four-story building. I'm on the work site and rush to him, but even I know it's too late.

I love my father, and it feels like my world is shattered with his body. The hardest part is telling my mother and brother, both sobbing like children with the news.

OVERNIGHT, I become the protector of the family.

I know that I have to find work on my own merit. Although people liked my father and would help me out of pity, pity only goes so far and for so long. I need to be hired because I can do the job. So I behave like my father. I do more than I am asked and stay longer than I am paid for.

At sixteen, but looking eighteen, I start to feed our family of three. I make my brother stay in school. I want him to have the future that my father and I had envisioned for our family.

My mother goes from house to house with a big basin to wash other people's clothes. At the end of the day, I see how red and swollen her hands are from the hard work. This is 1930s Poland, and being poor is just what most people are, but it's not what I would settle for.

I learn that if people like you, the chances of landing an odd job here or there are better. I practice looking in the mirror to perfect a pleasant look on my face—just enough friendliness and natural ease to be unassuming but confident.

Trying too hard scares people.

I start out mending the fence at a small cattle farm on the edge of town. Always willing to do whatever is asked, I soon become the guy to go to for solving problems. The owner notices me, and in six years I rise to become the general manager, despite being younger than most of the workers.

Cattle farms are full of men with rough dispositions, and fighting over minor slights is not uncommon. Rising to becoming manager had as much to do with my ability to herd men as cattle.

At six feet three inches tall and solid, I can handle anyone. In my actions I am fair, and the men above and below me know it.

Being manager has its privileges.

I bring my brother into the company to be the bookkeeper, and my mother no longer needs to wash the clothes of strangers. We have a nice house in town, and it looks like the future is bright.

Chapter 22

My mother, now having more time than she has ever had, begins to look for wives for her sons.

One Sunday, she is clearly excited as she tells us to wash up and put on our best clothes—that's a clean white shirt and black pants.

The matchmaker is bringing two sisters over to meet us.

My brother and I look at each other, and he says, "You can choose first."

I shouldn't have been surprised. Dawid is thoughtful, kind, and not too fussy.

As it turns out, we both find the girls to be very attractive. This can happen when all you see are men and cows, both covered in dirt, but truthfully the matchmaker earns her fee that day.

We learn later that it was difficult to find someone for the older sister because she had been married before and had a young son when her husband died.

We don't have to choose because it makes sense that the older sister marries me and the younger one my brother. I always wanted a son.

When Walter first comes to live with me, I'm not sure how it's going to work out. But being so young, he has few memories of his natural father to interfere with how he feels about me.

I didn't realize how much I would enjoy being a father.

Most people—who don't know—think that he is my son because he actually looks like me. We have the same sturdy build and our hair is a mop that's impossible to brush. We also both have a nose that you can't miss. He pinches mine and I pinch his while we both make honking donkey sounds. His mother pretends to be disgusted when we do this, but she has a smile when she says, "Stop that, you're not animals!"

Walter sticks to me like I did to my father, and he loves it when I take him to the farm, especially if I carry him on my shoulders.

My wife, Anelie, is a tough disciplinarian, which is a good thing because I can't be harsh with Walter. He's like my shadow when I come home. Our favorite game is when he pretends to be a wild bull that I have to catch and wrestle to the ground. He runs around the house yelling, "You can't catch me, you can't catch me," giggling as he darts around the furniture.

Anelie tells me that when it starts to get dark, Walter goes to sit on his stool by the window to wait for me. He looks for me to appear in the distance on the street so that even before I get to the house, the door flings open and he comes running right into me, yelling, "Papa, Papa." This becomes the highlight of my day.

My brother seems to have found someone perfect for him as well. While Anelie only speaks if she has something important to say, Bryda is very talkative and can keep us all entertained with stories of their day in the market, something funny that Walter did, or the latest gossip in town. She's more reliable than the newspaper, and her information is more accurate. She has quite the network of friends and contacts.

Our family of three goes to six in one step but feels like it was always meant to be that way.

My mother, for the first time, feels like her job is done.

Maybe she was holding on just for that. We never knew how sick she was, though for months she knew about the cancer. I'll always remember her final words: "Bronek, I wish your father could have seen how well you have done. He would have been so proud of you, as I am. A mother could not be luckier than to have both you and your brother for sons. I know that you'll look after everyone. I'm sorry to be leaving you, but it's my time."

In all of us, there is a child that exists while we have our parents.

With my mother gone, I feel a sadness for the loss of the child within myself.

Chapter 23

None of us know about the storm that is coming.

Only a year later, the world as we know it starts to change—gradually at first but then unbelievably so.

I am glad that my mother did not have to see what is happening.

The name Hitler is whispered among the Jews as Germany invades Poland on September 1, 1939. Equipped with guns, the Polish army is no match for the Germans, who come with tanks. Our country is easily defeated with just over a month of fighting.

Hitler and Stalin make a pact to support each other, and Poland is divided between them. It's a tense situation for everyone.

In our town the Bug River is the dividing line, with Germans on one side and Russians on the other. We live on the

Russian side and are thankful for that coincidence given stories we have heard of how the Nazis treat Jews.

This reprieve, however, does not last.

On a warm summer day in June 1941, the Germans break with the Russians and move to our side of town.

I look up at the clear blue sky, painted with soft clouds that float along, puzzled at how such tranquillity could exist in the natural world on such a day.

Chapter 24

At first there are restrictions on our activities, and we are required to wear a star to be identified. If you are identified as a Jew and don't wear the star visibly, you are shot on the spot and left on the side of the street.

Soon Jewish stores have to put signs in their windows so people know not to shop there.

Jews are also not allowed to work in certain industries and cannot shop in non-Jewish stores.

I keep working at the farm but am not surprised when the owner calls me in one day and says that he can no longer keep me.

He says that he has no choice, and I think he feels ashamed. Out of guilt or kindness, I guess it doesn't really matter; he pays me for three more months.

Being responsible for the family from a young age, I have

always been careful to have money set aside. Knowing that our belongings could be confiscated, I don't keep our money in the bank. I buy gold and bury manageable amounts in locations along the river. I do this late at night to make sure no one sees me. I have the locations committed to memory but make my family repeat over and over again where they are in case only one of us makes it. Having the gold helps us survive. Even gold from a Jew is welcomed in the black market for food and medicine.

Gold, since the beginning of time, has worked best.

From her contacts, Bryda tells us about the Zegota, an underground organization that provides false documents for Jews who can pass as Christians. The Zegota is funded by the Polish government in exile.

The problem is that Walter, Bryda, and I have classic Jewish features and cannot possibly pass for Christians. Anelie and Dawid can be disguised this way.

I try to persuade Dawid and Anelie to leave posing as a Christian couple, but they refuse, as I knew they would. "We stay together, Bronek. We're family." Dawid feels strongly about this.

I look woefully at my brother with the blond hair that has thinned out considerably. Always youthful in appearance, he now looks ten years older from worry. I know that I too have aged beyond my twenty-five years.

It is bad timing, but Anelie becomes pregnant in the midst of this.

We name our daughter Biata, meaning "blessed," and hope that her name will help to protect her.

Chapter 25

By September 1942, my gold is running low, and we are herded up and sent to live in a part of the city that has been sectioned off by barbed wire.

We are allowed to bring one bag each. I tell everyone to bring the most practical clothes and shoes. No one will care how we look. "We will need warm clothes and good walking shoes," I say.

Worried that they will search our bags and take our money, I have Anelie sew a false lining in the coats to hide our cash. Also, Walter's teddy bear has his stuffing replaced with zlotys.

My precaution pays off when our bags are searched on arrival. The Germans take everything valuable. They are ruthless and even have a dentist on hand to extract teeth for the gold fillings. We hear people begging and crying to keep their remaining possessions. I know that it's useless to plead with thugs, and that's how I see them. I could fight the bully in the schoolyard, but this is beyond anything that I can fix.

My family is given one room in an old house with seven other families. There are two small beds for the five of us. We keep a small pot under the bed for Walter, who can't wait for his turn to use the outhouse.

It's clear that the Germans want workers because they interview each of us, looking for skilled labor.

I am hired for a big industrial company that needs labor for a munitions factory. With my background in construction and my handiness with tools, I pass their test and am given working papers. Dawid does not. They're not interested in bookkeepers.

Surprisingly, the management of the factory treats everyone quite well, in contrast to the German soldiers. The rations for lunch are reasonable and consist of real food, not like the diluted soup and stale bread that we receive in the ghetto. I have a big appetite but always save some part of every meal for my family.

My papers keep us alive in other ways as well. They give me an opportunity to get to know the regular workers and gauge whom I can trust to trade with. When the supervisor is not looking, I pass the cash over and tuck the food coming back under my clothes.

The ghetto is guarded, but sparsely, so I sneak out late at night by timing the rotation of the guards. There are areas where the ground is lower, and by lifting the barbed wire with a metal bar, I can slide under. It's a good thing I know the route to the river by heart because I have to dig up what gold is left in the dark. This is my backup when all the cash is gone.

Chapter 26

All around us, people are thinner by the day. We see hopelessness in the faces of people we pass in the street and we try not to look at anyone because they are begging for help. Sanitation is poor, and with the overcrowding, disease is rampant. Rats are healthier than people in the ghetto.

With the finish line being death, it is a race between disease and hunger for most people.

Incredibly, despite the harsh conditions, Walter makes friends easily. I see him running and playing with the other children when I come back from work. He still gives me the hug that I look forward to every day.

On Chanukah, I am excited to give Walter a piece of cake hidden in my handkerchief from a trade at work. It was more than I could really spare, so there will be meager rations for dinner, but we all wanted to make this sacrifice for

Walter. His eyes light up when he sees the cake, but he doesn't eat it right away, as I thought he would. He puts it carefully away in his pocket.

I say to him, "Walter, don't you want to eat it?"

He says, "It looks so good, Papa, and I really want to."

"Then go ahead," I say. "It's all yours."

It is a regular piece of cake, but he hasn't seen one in months and says, "It's so big, Papa, and I love it, but my friend Sari has never had anything this special, and I want to share it with her tomorrow."

My first thought is, *Don't you know how hard it was for me to get this for you? Don't you know that we're all starving and that you should hoard what you can for yourself and your family?*

Deep inside of me, though, there is a part that is very proud of him. Without the war in the backdrop, I would have said, "Walter, that is very kind, and I am proud of you."

But there is a war, and his survival might depend on being selfish one day. What to do as his father?

I say, "Sari is lucky to have a friend like you," and the beautiful smile that comes back tells me that I did the right thing.

I decide that his character is worth more than the price of the cake.

I don't want the war to diminish Walter as it has done to the rest of us.

Chapter 27

One day, a German officer gathers us in the open square within the ghetto and announces that they need workers for a brick factory. No experience is required and the workers will be given food for their families. This is the best news we have heard in some time.

My brother and I look at each other. Very quietly he says to me, "We don't know if this is true or not. Only one of us should go."

I have to agree.

He continues. "You already have a job, Bronek. I should go." He doesn't have to say what else is on his mind because I already know what he is thinking: *I trust you to protect the family.* His thoughts remind me of my mother.

That night, Ely, one of the men who works with me at the

factory, comes to our house. His voice is shaky when he asks, "Bronek, can I speak to you privately?"

I answer, "Yes, of course," and we walk over to a quiet corner in the room.

He says, "I can't feed my family. I am watching my wife and daughter slowly starve to death. You know they only give us enough food to feed ourselves at the factory. I can't save enough to keep us all alive for much longer. If I could go to this brick factory and get enough food for my family, it would really make a difference. Can you help me, Bronek? Can you tell the supervisor tomorrow that I was sick and couldn't make it? They will believe it if you tell them."

At the factory, I had become the unspoken leader for the Jews from the ghetto. Whenever the supervisor needed anything done, he came to me and I organized the jobs. I conveyed a sense of confidence that I didn't have but knew was essential.

What Ely was asking was dangerous and would risk my position at the factory if we were found out. I wanted to help him, but I couldn't. It was not because I was afraid of what would happen to me. It was what would happen to my family without me.

"I'm sorry, Ely. I want to help you, but I can't."

He doesn't answer; he just looks at me with hope that I will change my mind, and that's worse.

As I see the slumped shoulders and the fragile frame of a good man leaving my house, I think I should run after him and tell him, "Yes, I will help you," but I don't.

Early the next morning, we go to the pickup spot in the square. There is already a large crowd of men anxiously waiting.

Dawid whispers to me, "I hope they can take everyone."

When the trucks arrive, men are shoving each other to get to the front of the line. The brick factory is outside of town, so it will be late when they return. From the square, I wave to Dawid and then walk with some of the men to our job.

Ely walks with us and doesn't look at me.

Someone says, "Life is hard."

I agree, but what's the alternative?

WHEN I RETURN that evening, the sun has already gone down.

Many of us gather in the square to wait for the trucks to return. Although no one says a word, you can feel the tension as time goes by.

It's dark when the silence is broken by the sound of the siren that signals curfew. Everyone has to go home. That's when we hear the guttural wail of a desperate woman. It's a sound that can only come from agony, sorrow, and despair.

We have all been betrayed.

There are no trucks returning.

My eyes water, and then uncontrollable sobs break from my body. My knees give, and I sink to the earth. It feels like someone has torn the limbs from my body. I can hardly breathe. The crying and hysteria all around me seem like background noise.

Chapter 28

It's not until later that we find out the truth.

There are people who come to the ghetto to trade for food and medicine. Their prices are steep, but they justify this by the risk they take and the bribes they pay.

One of the traders tells us what really happened. "Don't you know that the brick factory was bombed months ago? Your brother and the rest of the men were lined up against the wall and shot. Their bodies are still there with the broken bricks."

Oh, Dawid, this is not how we envisioned our lives would end, and it suddenly hits me that I must move quickly. Time is running out.

I need to get the rest of my family out of here. *Think clearly; don't panic*, I say to myself. *Find a place to hide*.

I know at least twenty men who have worked for me. I am

also close to the owner of the farm. I need to find someone who will help us.

Why didn't I think of this earlier? I ask myself this question over and over again because it might have meant saving my brother. But guilt is a luxury I cannot afford while my family still needs me, so I shrug it off.

During the day, I walk as close to the edge of the ghetto as I can without arousing suspicion.

Is there a place for all of us to escape?

I need to find a spot that is not too far from where we are living, since it is dangerous to be out past curfew.

I also need a location where the guards have less focus. My usual exit is too far for my family to make it by hiding in between the shadows of the buildings.

After sizing up the situation, I realize that there is no choice but to cut the barbed wire to make our exit close to the house. Since we will never be using that escape route again, it won't matter that the guards see it the next day and realize that we have escaped. It's not good for the people left behind, but we can't think that far.

Late at night, I continue to sneak out where the ground is lower.

I am careful because sneaking out of the ghetto is punishable by death. In fact, soldiers are instructed to shoot anyone who even looks like he is trying to escape. If I die, I know that Walter, Anelie, Biata, and Bryda have no chance.

Risking all of our lives each night, I visit the homes of my friends.

The stories are unique, but the pattern is the same.

"You know I want to help you and your family, but we can't risk it."

Everyone is sorry, but no one is sorry enough.

The penalty for hiding Jews is death—not just to you, but to your entire family.

In many ways, I could not blame them—even if I wanted to.

Chapter 29

One night, I am sliding under the barbed wire again when a German soldier unexpectedly comes around the corner of a nearby building. I freeze and am almost sure that our eyes meet, but it's dark. For some reason, he turns around to walk in the direction that he has just come from.

I am shocked. Did he not see me?

I keep going. What choice do I have?

It feels like a small lift to evade the soldier, but I don't feel too victorious because this is my last chance.

I have exhausted every friendship.

Almost begging my friend, I do the one thing that I know scares people.

I sound desperate.

I can't help it because I am so very desperate at this point.

My friend is practically pushing me out the door for fear that someone might see me at his house.

Walking back toward the ghetto, I think of Ely and feel all alone in the world.

I walk along the river, where there is light reflected from the moon.

I start talking to my mother.

I say that I have no more ideas and that I need help. I turn to my mother as I would have done when I was a young child.

I am walking past something familiar, Street of Our Lady, and then it hits me.

This is the street that Franciszka lives on.

Franciszka is a woman who raises chickens and grows vegetables on her small piece of land.

We met her a few years ago when my brother and I, in our wagon, saw her walking with a basket of eggs and a heavy sack of vegetables to sell in the market. She smiled up at us, and even though it came from an old body, her eyes were vibrant and full of energy.

We made room and gave her a ride.

From then on, she waited for us every week when we went into town for supplies.

She gave us carrots because she was a proud woman and didn't want a free ride.

I KNOCK ON HER DOOR.

It must have been sometime around two in the morning. I don't know what I expected. I knew her, but only superficially.

After a few minutes, a familiar voice comes through the wooden door. "Who is it?"

"It's Bronek, Franciszka."

She opens the door quickly and ushers me in.

She whispers, "My daughter is asleep."

I look at her. How funny that I used to think of her as a poor woman living in this small wooden house. She looks like a queen in a castle to me now. What I would have given to be able to live here with my family.

I look at those eyes and say, "Do you remember me, Franciszka?"

She says, "Yes, of course. You and your brother."

Her voice is purposely low, so I continue in a whisper as well.

"Franciszka, Dawid is dead. He was shot by the Germans. Please help us. We have nowhere else to go. You are my last hope."

I tell her that I have a wife, two children, and a sister-in-law.

Bronek

PEOPLE ARE LIKE WATER in a pond where you cannot see the bottom. You think you know where it is shallow and where it is deep, but it's only when you have to dive in head-first that you find out where it is truly deep.

These are unreasonable times with severe punishment for providing help, however small, to a Jew. Giving a piece of bread or water to a Jew has become a death sentence in Poland.

Knowing this, Franciszka, a woman I barely know, agrees to hide us above her pigsty in the animal shed attached to her house.

I can't believe it.

I was not expecting such a response.

She has an idea to use hay as a barrier that we can hide behind.

"Give me a week to clear out the space slowly, so no one will be suspicious," she says.

I feel that there is goodness in the world after all, and it's embodied in this small, white-haired woman sitting in front of me.

"What about your daughter?" Perhaps that is why we are whispering.

"She'll be fine. She's like me." I take that to mean that compassion is a family trait.

I run back to the ghetto. A man with hope moves differently than one without—so I am floating all the way.

The moon seems brighter, and I am certain there are more stars in the sky than before I met Franciszka.

Chapter 30

The next morning, we are awakened by screaming and gunshots.

There is a raid on the ghetto.

They are rounding people up in the same trucks that took my brother.

I know what this means.

I take my son and hide him in a woodshed, telling him to stay quiet until I return. Only six, he understands that his survival depends on it.

My wife, sister-in-law, and I, with the baby in one arm, climb a steep ladder leading to the small opening of an attic.

There is pandemonium below.

Then the baby starts to cry.

My wife looks at me with helpless panic. She tries to rock Biata and cradles her against her chest, but nothing works.

We had moved the ladder away from the entrance of the attic to deflect attention, but someone is moving it back and climbing up—someone who speaks German.

It's a Polish police officer working with a German soldier below. He looks at my terrified wife and whispers, "Do you want to go with your baby?"

She only has a minute to make a decision that no one could make in a lifetime.

She gives him our baby.

Descending the stairs, he says to the German soldier that he has found an abandoned baby.

"Doesn't matter," says the soldier. "We'll get the mother later."

I think that had it not been for our son, she would have gone with our baby.

We stay hidden for a while even after the noise has died down and all the trucks have gone.

We know that you can never be too careful.

How do you move when you feel like you can't go on?

You think of someone who needs you more.

We find our son asleep in the woodshed, and we move on.

In the middle of the night again, I make the trip to Street of Our Lady with my wife, her sister, and my son, all so solemn now that you would think we were going to our death.

Walter whispers to me, "I saw them take Biata, Papa. Will they come for me too?"

I look down at the angelic face asking me a question that no child should ever have to ask, and I say to him, "I will never let that happen, Walter."

Franciszka is surprised to see us, and although she is not ready, she does not turn us away.

I help clear out the upper loft, and we move in.

She asks about the baby, and when I tell her what happened, she lets out the loudest wail.

We are all touched by her reaction, but at the same time we hope no one heard her cry.

I have nothing to offer Franciszka for taking us in, and I remember all the times that we took her carrots for the wagon ride.

Chapter 31

Franciszka keeps three pigs in the shed, and this is more clever than you might imagine. Pigs make noise and that covers up mistakes that we make, such as coughing, sneezing, and even talking, which can be heard by a visiting neighbor.

The German soldiers don't know who is Jewish, and they don't know who would be hiding them. It would be a neighbor or a friend who would give you away for a small reward.

Franciszka cooks all the food in one pot and takes it out to the shed, as if she is feeding the pigs.

To cover our waste, she mixes it with the waste from the pigs and shovels it out.

I see Franciszka with enlightened eyes now. This is the savviest woman I have ever known.

One night, she tells us that she is having a dinner party for some Germans and that we need to be especially quiet. Dinner for Germans? She has chutzpah.

That night we are all terrified to breathe. We hear music coming through the walls of the house, and although it is a refreshing break from the constant noises made by the pigs, we are on pins and needles and have a hard time enjoying it. What seems like an eternity later, the sounds die down and Franciszka comes through the shed with a pot of leftovers. In that pot is the most delicious sauerkraut that I have ever tasted.

TO PASS THE TIME, we play cards, and I teach Walter to play chess. It's not a time for frivolous purchases, but Helena uses some of the money she earns from her job to buy this game for him. It seems so unreal to me that these kind people could be executed for helping us.

I teach Walter various strategies, and he's a quick learner. The happiest moment of his deprived childhood is when he beats me at chess one day. We learn not to speak, but I can read his joy by the big smile on his face. It's both touching and sad to me.

He deserves so much more than this.

Anelie carries the memory of Biata with her constantly and is not able to get over the guilt. She has nightmares and we are afraid that she will shout out in her sleep. Bryda never recovers from the loss of Dawid either, but she doesn't have the emotional breakdown that Anelie suffers.

We take turns watching over Anelie while she sleeps to make sure there are no outbursts that would give us away. I miss Dawid as well, but feeling sorry for myself won't help my family, so I refuse to let those feelings in. When I close my eyes I focus on happy memories of him before the war.

It's very tight in the loft, and most of the time we spend just sitting. We take turns massaging each other's legs and shoulders so they won't become stiff. We don't speak. Walter tells me things with hand gestures, and we create our own language this way.

There is a small window in the loft, where we can peek out from behind the heavy curtain. We rotate spots so that someone can sit beside the window each day. It's important to have something to look forward to, however small.

From the window, we can see the apple tree that Helena told us her brother planted.

When the apples begin to ripen, she picks them for us.

We know it's very special.

Walter likes to count the apples on the tree. We compare

our numbers and spend hours verifying who is right. Although it's just something to pass the time, it's still a game. We make up games to keep Walter as amused as possible.

One of our favorites started when I did a shadow puppet on the wall. This game is played with animal shadows created from our hands and fingers.

We don't know where she got it, but Helena gives Walter a piece of chocolate for no particular reason. Walter looks at me for approval and when I nod, he gives her a big hug and thanks her in a whisper.

He looks at his treasure, not believing it. If he could jump up and down, he would have.

She looks genuinely happy at his response.

We turn down Walter's offer to share and watch with amusement as he breaks off a fingernail piece to enjoy each day.

Chapter 32

One day, we see Helena crying under her tree and don't know why.

Later, Franciszka tells us that her son was killed.

We know that Damian was responsible for helping to feed us and, although we only met him a few times, we were grateful to him.

There is so much sorrow everywhere.

Anelie and Bryda start crying, but even then we have to be careful not to be heard.

I promise myself that if we survive this, I will never forget what Franciszka and her family have sacrificed for us.

At the beginning of the war, no one believed that the Germans, a civilized people, would enforce mass executions of the Jewish people, as they have done. We thought that hiding with Franciszka would be temporary and short, but now it's been over a year.

We live each moment not knowing if it will be our last.

We live with constant fear, but we have to fight the boredom that is each day as well. Boredom can make you careless, and I stay alert not to let this happen.

THE SITUATION BECOMES quite alarming when German soldiers park their tanks right outside the shed. Luckily, a smelly pigsty is not inviting for most people. It doesn't bother us because we have become accustomed to the smell and don't even notice it.

Franciszka purposely does not shovel out the waste from the pigs too often, knowing that German soldiers take great pride in their shiny boots and would not likely want to walk into a dirty pigsty. You never know, though, and seeing those uniforms so close is unnerving.

We are so terrified that we don't dare peek out of the curtain.

Walter cuddles up to me, and I know he is scared like the rest of us.

Part III

MIKOLAJ

Chapter 33

My father is a doctor and the head of the hospital. People bow when they see him.

He believes that because of his position and his importance in the community, he doesn't have to worry about being Jewish.

My father is a smart man, but he is wrong.

By the time he realizes this, it's too late for us to escape.

My mother is a beautiful woman who has lived a life of privilege all her thirty years.

Like everyone else, she defers to my father, who makes all the decisions. But, for the first time, my father does not know what to do. It hits him very hard.

My mother is about eight years younger than my father. She is the daughter of his professor, and my father met her when he, along with six other students, was invited over to their home for dinner.

I have heard this story from my mother a hundred times. I think that she likes to replay it in her mind.

My mother says, "Your father showed up and I thought he was the most handsome man that I had ever seen, but I was just a young girl and quite awkward in front of him.

"After dinner, my father asked me to play the piano and sing for our guests. I was quite nervous, but I sang a traditional Polish song that most people would know. I could see your father's face transform with delight as I sang. I didn't know, but it was one of his favorite songs and one that his mother sang to him as a child.

"After I finished singing, he stood up and enthusiastically started to clap. This is unusual for your father. You know how reserved he is, and it was funny because he found himself standing all alone for a few seconds before the rest of the guests realized what had happened and stood up as well.

"After that, your father always found a reason to come by the house. Maybe it was to clarify a point in class or for some feedback on a paper he was writing.

"Your grandfather finally asked if he would like to court me, and your father's answer was that he would like that very much.

"For the next year, your father came over every Sunday. We would go for walks in the park or he would listen to me play the piano. It was all very formal and always with a chaperone.

"When your father finally graduated at the top of his class and was offered a position at the hospital in Sokal, your grandfather gave his consent for him to marry me.

"He told your grandfather that he would always look after me.

"As you can see, Mikolaj, he keeps his promises." My mother wants to point this out to me.

"I went from having servants to look after the cooking, cleaning, and shopping at home, to having different ones to do the same thing when I married your father."

I know that my father dotes on my mother, bringing home beautiful dresses and jewelry for no particular reason.

She tells him that she loves everything he buys her because this makes him happy.

Secretly, she gives away some of her dresses. She says to me, "They're nice, but not all of them are really my taste."

She knows I won't tell.

One day, my father sees a young woman in town wearing the exact same dress that he had just given to my mother. When he comes home that night, he says, "Felicia, it was the same dress that I bought you, but I know that it would have looked much better on you."

He never asks my mother if it was her dress that the young woman was wearing.

That is just my father.

Chapter 34

My father's reputation grew and, with it, his position at the hospital. He felt that he next needed a family to be complete.

Five years after they were married, they anxiously received me into the world.

The best nurses were hired to be on hand weeks ahead.

My mother, at twenty-two, was considered old for being a first-time mother.

"The day you were born was the happiest day of my life," my mother often tells me.

Because my mother is home all day, she tells me stories. That's my favorite, her stories.

Sometimes at night, when I can't fall asleep, she asks me to close my eyes and then magically transports me to faraway places with her words. There are pirates looking for treasure, princes rescuing damsels, and dragons to be tamed.

My mother is the most beautiful of all the mothers. When we have big dinner parties, it's clear that my father is very proud of her.

Like her father, my father asks her to play the piano for everyone, but never to sing. It was her singing that made him fall in love with her, and he feels that it is private.

I feel privileged that my mother sings to me all day, when we are on our own.

Chapter 35

Every night after dinner, my father reads us a passage from his medical journal. He wants my mother and me to be well informed.

One evening, he reads that eggs are good for the mental and physical development of children.

The very next day, my mother and I make a trip to the market looking for fresh eggs. We find this old woman, who brings them in from her little farm on the edge of town.

My mother thinks that Franciszka is sweet because she doesn't mind me playing with the eggs, which makes most of the other merchants upset. People don't realize that the path to my mother's heart passes through me.

So we buy a dozen eggs from her and put them in our basket to take home.

On the way, there is an argument in the market when two

vendors are fighting over a space. The shouting becomes shoving, which becomes fighting. A crowd gathers, and it pushes us forward.

My mother and I are terrified, and, standing too close, she is pushed over when one of the men falls back. All the eggs go flying out of the basket, so that both of us are dripping and covered with broken eggshells as we rush home.

When my father hears what happened, he is furious.

"You never go to the market," he says. "That is what we have servants for."

But my mother likes Franciszka and has told her that she would buy eggs from her the following week.

Very cleverly, my mother asks our cook to find Franciszka at the market and to bring her to our house instead.

I think my mother liked having someone new to talk to, and, as hard as it is to explain, she made a connection with Franciszka.

ON ONE OF HER VISITS, we notice that Franciszka seems a little distracted.

My mother asks, "Is there something bothering you?"

She tells us that her daughter is very beautiful and smart

but there are many candidates applying for the job she is interviewing for.

Franciszka says, "I worry that they won't hire her because her clothes are not fancy enough."

My mother says, "Well, we can solve that problem," and she disappears into her room and comes back with two dresses.

"Do you think these will fit her?"

Franciszka looks somewhat confused at my mother. "Yes, you're both slim, so they should fit her well. I just need to take up the hem a bit since you are taller than Helena, but that's easy to fix. It's just that . . ." She pauses. "It's just that I can't really afford to buy them from you."

My mother responds with a giggle. "Oh no, you can have them. I have so many that I could never wear them all anyway. Besides, this vanilla dress is particularly suited for someone working in an office. When would I ever wear that at home with Mikolaj?" she says, as she ruffles my hair.

And so it must have been Franciszka's daughter that my father saw that day.

Both my mother and I knew this.

We are excited when Franciszka tells us that her daughter, Helena, got the job.

Chapter 36

After the Germans come to Poland, my father still works at the hospital but is demoted from chief.

One day, a German commander comes to the hospital with an appendix that has burst.

"He could have died," my father tells us.

The commander needs an operation immediately and demands, "Who is your best surgeon?"

"That would be Dr. Wolenski" is the response. "But he is Jewish."

The commander says, "Get him for me now!"

My father says, "I guess when your life is on the line, you can turn your head the other way, because the commander orders me to do the operation. He also instructs his guard to shoot me if he doesn't survive."

My mother and I gasp, but then my father says, "Don't worry. As you can see, I am here to tell you the story, so there's a happy ending. I saved him."

My father regularly checks on his patient, and a kind of uneasy friendship develops between them.

"It's hard not to have a high regard for your father," my mother says, and I know what she means.

A short time after this, my father is told that he can no longer work at the hospital.

His dedication, his reputation, and his leadership—none of it mattered.

The commander is not as bad as we think because after he leaves the hospital, he comes to see my father at home. He tells us to sell whatever we can and to get out. He says that within months, all the Jews in Sokal will be rounded up and kept in an enclosed area that they are mapping out. "I cannot help you any more than this," he says.

My father thanks him, and they shake hands before he leaves.

MY PARENTS START to sell everything—our furniture, our paintings, our clothes, and even our house. My mother complains that people are paying us a fraction of what our things are worth, but my father says, "We don't have a choice and the buyers know it."

I hear my father telling my mother that he has false passports, but no one will take the chance to transport us because he is too well recognized. "Maybe you and Mikolaj should go without me," he says.

My mother is torn between my safety and leaving my father. In the end, she says, "We can't go without you, Helmut," and that is the first time I see my father cry.

"If we can't leave, then we must hide," my father says. He starts to approach the other doctors and nurses from the hospital.

I remember that we have many friends, from all the people who came to our parties.

My mother says to me privately, "It's not easy for your father to ask for help. He's used to other people asking him for help."

As the days pass, my father looks more discouraged. Even though they are in the profession of saving lives, none of his colleagues are willing to provide us with refuge.

By now, I am not allowed to go to school anymore, and it's just the three of us at home.

All our help have left as well.

I always thought it would be wonderful not to have to go to school and to have both my parents at home with me, but this is not how I imagined it would be.

Chapter 37

"Why do people hate us so much, Mama?" I ask.

My mother says, "Do you remember what you said when you were a little boy, and you tripped on the street?"

I shook my head because I couldn't remember.

"You had fallen and were embarrassed, so you said that an ant tripped you. Do you think that an ant could have tripped you?"

"No, of course not," I answer.

"Well, to Hitler, we're the ant. He has many people believing that Jews are the cause of their troubles, but he hasn't fooled everyone. You know Franciszka is smarter than that, right? Well, there are others too."

My mother's words are comforting.

Chapter 38

After all our servants have left, Franciszka still comes with her fresh eggs and vegetables. My mother says, "There is some decency in the world after all."

Franciszka comes even though she knows we're Jewish, and, unlike the others, she doesn't charge us double for doing so.

One day, my mother is talking to Franciszka, and she lowers her voice the way she does when she doesn't want me to hear what she is saying to my father.

"Can you hide us? We have money. We can pay you."

Franciszka takes a moment to think and then says, "I only have two rooms in my house. One is the kitchen and the other is a bedroom that I share with my daughter. There is nowhere to hide, unless . . ." and then she lowers her voice so quietly that now I can't hear a thing.

My mother calls out to my father, "Helmut, come quickly."

They huddle and speak with great animation. My father nods in agreement and Franciszka gets up to leave.

For the next several weeks, my father sleeps all morning and doesn't play with me until the afternoon.

One night, my mother wakes me up and we walk in the dark along the river.

I am really tired, but my mother says that it's important to keep walking.

My father leads the way and seems to know where to go even though it's hard to see anything.

Finally, when we arrive, it turns out to be where Franciszka lives.

I am so tired that I want to sleep in the bed as soon as we arrive.

My mother says that we have to wait while my father and Franciszka move her kitchen table, the rug underneath, and then a wooden plank to reveal a small cellar below.

It's dark and small, and I don't want to go down there. But my mother takes my hand and says, "We're playing hide-and-seek with the Germans, and they'll never find us here."

Over the past weeks, my father, with surgeon's hands, had dug this hole under the kitchen in the middle of the night to make a shelter for us.

He brought cash and provisions to be stored in our hideaway with each trip. There were books, candles, dry food, and medicine, as well as precious pictures of our family.

The timing was close.

A few weeks later, all the Jews were rounded up and placed in a confined area.

For all the lives that my father saved, and the thought that we might have been repaid in kind, it was my mother's friendship with Franciszka that gave us a chance.

Chapter 39

We have to be very quiet during the day because you never know if a neighbor will drop by.

One day Franciszka tells us about a Polish family that was found to have hidden Jews. They were forced to walk throughout the village with signs describing their crime before they were hanged in the public square as an example.

This shakes us all up.

A Polish pharmacist had turned them in. He suspected that the family was hiding Jews when they purchased more medicine than they usually would have needed.

Not all Nazis are German.

My father says to Franciszka, "We will never forget what you and your daughter have done for us. The war will be over one day, and we will repay you."

She says, "It's wrong, what is happening. I'm only doing what is decent."

She says to my mother, "You would do the same for me," and my mother nods, although who really knows? Would my mother have been willing to risk my life?

Chapter 40

One day, the deliveryman comes to drop off a notice from German headquarters.

There is now a reward of five liters of whiskey and some cash for turning in a Jew.

He calls out to Franciszka, and she opens the door.

At this exact moment, I sneeze.

It is damp in the cellar, and I have caught a very bad cold. My father is worried but does not have cough syrup, even though he brought other medicines. We all agreed that it was not possible to obtain medicine discreetly, especially from the infamous pharmacist.

The deliveryman pushes past Franciszka and comes in.

He sees that there is no one in the house.

We hear him accusing Franciszka. "You're hiding someone, aren't you? I'm sure I heard something. I'm going to report you."

To the astonishment of Franciszka and the deliveryman, there is a knock from the floor.

Franciszka is frozen. She doesn't know what to do now.

Then the knock becomes louder.

The deliveryman says, "Franciszka, someone hiding under your floor wants to come out."

They move the kitchen table, and my father emerges from under the floor.

He says to the deliveryman, "Hello, Leszek."

My father's voice is deep and resonates with authority.

He speaks as if there is no war, as if there is no hunt for Jews, and as if he is still the chief at the hospital.

For a moment, we are all suspended in this reality.

My father then says, "How is your wife, Edyta?"

He had saved her life.

The man is clearly taken aback here. "Dr. Wolenski, I didn't know it was you. Of course I won't say anything."

My father continues as if this man has come for a visit. "Good, now if you or your family need medical care, you can come here, and I will personally look after you."

"Yes, yes, thank you very much, Doctor." Leszek sounds like a different man than the one we heard earlier.

"Before you go," my father says, "I need you to buy some medicine for my son who you heard coughing. Here is fifty zlotys for the cough medicine. You will need to say that it is for your wife. Understood?"

"Yes, Doctor, of course. I will bring it tomorrow," Leszek replies.

We can hear my father's command of the situation from our hiding place, but my mother and I do not come out.

We huddle together like two little mice.

After Leszek leaves, my father returns to us and the table is replaced over our heads.

He is shaking, and my mother goes to him.

She holds him the way she holds me when I have had a bad dream.

The next day, good as his word, Leszek returns with the cough medicine.

We all know that cough medicine costs a few zlotys, but we weren't expecting any change.

Chapter 41

Every day is night, so I dream of seeing the sun.

I remember the warmth of it shining through the window onto my face in my bedroom. How could I ever have found that annoying, and why did I close the blinds to go back to sleep?

We have a daily ritual, my mother and I. She tells me to close my eyes as she paints beautiful pictures in my mind with her words, like she used to. Mesmerizing me with her voice, it often starts like this: "You are sleeping in your bed, and the sun is shining through your window, so you are sleeping in later this day. I wake you as we are about to have a big breakfast together. Papa, you, and I are sitting at our dining-room table, and we are eating scrambled eggs with toast and jam. We drink lots and lots of milk. We are so full now that we cannot eat another bite. You pack your books for school, and you give me a big hug before going off on your day."

We don't dream of exotic trips or adventures anymore.

We dream of our old life, and of our routines. We long to return to the world as we remembered it.

I see that my father closes his eyes when my mother works her visual magic.

He is soaking it all up, like I am.

IN OUR PREVIOUS LIFE, our world revolved around my father.

It seemed like my mother and I were just playing around until he came home.

At the dinner table, we would hear about his patients, his operations, his views on politics, and so on.

In our hiding place, my father is very quiet.

Once in a while, through the dim lighting of a small lamp, I see him smile at me, but not much more.

My mother, on the other hand, is always thinking of something for us to do. We have lessons in Yiddish. We do math problems from worksheets. It is endless activity.

My father made sure there were many books for me to learn from.

I see my mother brush my father's hair, something I have never seen before.

She tells us that we must be well prepared because one day we will leave Poland and go to Palestine.

She has no doubt that we will all go there together and rebuild our life. "Helmut, you will again be the great doctor that you are, and Mikolaj, you will go to school there."

Her absolute certainty gives us hope and strength.

I always thought that my mother could not live without my father, but it was the other way around.

I hear my father say to my mother one day, "You are my *bashert.*"

When my father is asleep, I whisper to my mother, "What is a *bashert?*"

She says, "*Bashert* is a very special word in Yiddish. It means 'soul mate.' It means 'destiny.' If you find your *bashert,* it means that you have found the person that you were meant to be with—the person that completes you. It is the finest thing that your father could have said to me."

"Do you think I will be able to find my *bashert,* Mama?" I am worried. What if we never get out of here?

She says, "Mikolaj, there is someone out there who is waiting to find you too. Maybe she is hiding, just like us. One day, we will all be free to find each other. I am sure of it."

That makes me feel better.

Chapter 42

Franciszka buys food and asks for it to be wrapped in newspapers instead of a paper bag. She doesn't read, so buying a newspaper would be suspicious. She feeds my father with day-old news, and he looks forward to those papers as much as the food that they wrap.

When Franciszka first tells my parents that she is inviting the German commander over for dinner, my mother is nervous and says, "Oh, is that safe?"

My father finds it ironic that we are hiding right beneath where they will be eating.

The day of the dinner, the smells are wonderful and make us even hungrier. My mother said to me the night before that I would need to be patient because Franciszka would make enough for us too.

In our space under the table, we can hear the sounds of the party above.

My father nods when he hears the commander speak because he knows that voice.

It is strange to hear the soldiers sing and laugh because whenever we saw them before, they were always serious and scary.

MANY DAYS LATER and quite unexpectedly, we hear the news about Damian.

We feel the weight of the grief above us, and my father shakes his head in pity.

My mother holds me close as if she might lose her son at any time too.

Part IV

Vilheim

Chapter 43

I am lucky not to have been born earlier in Germany.

Having turned eighteen in 1942, I am not recruited until the war has been going on for almost three years.

My commanders think that I am useless, but they don't know that I shoot to miss.

I can't imagine taking a life, any life.

Before being drafted into the army, I had hoped to become a veterinarian. My *oma* has a dairy farm, which has been in our family for a hundred years. The farm is located in the far north of Germany, where there are more cows than people. Unlike other farms, we also keep horses, goats, and pigs.

The land here is as beautiful as you will see anywhere, with green pastures stretching to meet the horizon. Even with the war, it feels peaceful here.

Oma teaches me to value every living being—an attitude that is sorely inconsistent with being a soldier and a Nazi.

MY PARENTS DIVORCED SHORTLY after my birth, so I have never seen them both together, except in a few pictures that Oma has. They're both attractive people with perfect smiles.

My mother wanted to pursue an acting career and felt that if anyone knew that she had a child, it would have made her less attractive, less desirable. She left me with her mother, who loves me enough to make up for both my mother and my father.

I have no memories of my father because he visited only once when I was still a baby.

The earliest memory I have of my mother is that she came to visit on a rainy day.

I know because I was wet and when I went to hug her, as Oma had instructed me to do, my mother pushed me away and said, "Oh no, not my silk dress. You'll ruin it!"

Her usual way with me is to say, "Kiss, kiss," like it is one word, while sending puckering sounds in my direction.

Sometimes she puts her cheek against mine while she kisses into the air and says, "I love you, darling."

"It's hard for your mother, Vilheim, because you look so much like your father," Oma tells me.

I picture myself looking like Oma and not my father, who I don't think much about. Both Oma and I are tanned and toned from spending so much time outdoors. My mother, by comparison, has skin so pale, it's almost translucent. When I was small, I used to think that she might have been a ghost, and I was afraid of her.

I learn that when my mother comes to visit, one of our animals will soon be gone. She needs money and Oma has to sell a horse, some goats, or some pigs to give her the cash she has come for.

It becomes so obvious to me that I resent her visits. I start to hate her beauty, her floral perfume, her furs, and everything about her.

I run to hide when she comes, afraid that she might take me with her.

She never does.

Eventually my mother stops coming to visit at all, and we hear that she has gone to the United States.

I am relieved that our animals are now safe.

Chapter 44

Oma and I eat very little meat.

It happened one day while we were having lamb for dinner.

We looked out the window at our sheep, who were peacefully grazing on the hill. They were so innocent and beautiful. In that moment, we both looked at each other and then down at our plates. It just felt wrong.

I learn how to take care of all the animals and even have my own horse. I spend hours brushing and grooming him, and, unlike most people, I look forward to it.

On my horse, I ride through fields and forests, which are oblivious to the ambitions of men.

It is when I feel the most free.

From when I was quite young, my *oma* has said to me,

"Vilheim, all this will be yours one day, and you must know how to look after it."

I feel a great responsibility toward all the animals.

I won't be like my father or mother, who don't care about anyone but themselves.

Chapter 45

Oma looks very serious one evening as we sit by the fireplace after dinner.

She has dismissed all the farm workers early and asked that we not be disturbed.

"Vilheim," she says solemnly, "Germany started a war and although we are far from it on our farm, it will come for you.

"You'll be asked to kill people you don't know, and the opposite will be true too.

"Survive this by keeping your head down. Avoid as much as you can. Do not be brave. This is not a war of necessity or principle."

I understand—play along.

Oma warns me, "Trust no one."

I know that her words are enough to have her shot for treason.

"You must live and you must come back to me, Vilheim. I have no one else. If you die, I die."

I listen to her and nod.

It's heartbreaking.

Chapter 46

The day I turn eighteen, the army reaches out and pulls me into it.

Oma packs my favorite foods and tells me over and over again that she loves me.

It's terrible from the first day.

The army crushes gentle souls.

My poor performance during training is the reason I am sent to a place where no one wants to go. I take comfort in thinking that there are no good places.

I am sent to Poland, so that we'll be ready to move into Russia when the order comes.

I dread that.

When I arrive in Poland, I am sent to Sokal, a town I never even knew existed. It's a small town, and that works better for me. Not far from town, there are pastures, which remind me of home. I know that I must never let my true feelings show, so I learn to follow orders with a serious expression on my face. My new commander thinks that I am a most conscientious young man. He's reading me all wrong, but I keep it up.

When I arrive, I am given the job of patrolling the ghetto. I really hate doing this because I am instructed to shoot anyone trying to escape.

I feel like such an imposter.

If I could set these people free, I would.

ONE NIGHT, while I am patrolling the inside perimeter of the ghetto, I round the corner of a building and happen to see a man trying to slide under the wire. It's too late for me to look away and our eyes meet. It's dark, but we both know that we saw each other. I am about to bring my rifle down from blind training, but I don't. I turn and pretend that I never saw him. A few minutes later, enough time for him to have made it across, I resume my patrol.

I wished him well.

I don't know why we are holding all these Jews in this confined area. I never even met a Jewish person before I entered the army. It makes no sense to me whatsoever. How can a war be based on persecuting innocent people?

Then, the orders come.

We are to deport all the people in the ghetto to concentration camps.

I hear that they will be executed there.

It is sickening and I want no part of it, but there is nothing I can do—if I don't want to be executed myself.

That day is one of the most horrible of my life.

There is chaos everywhere.

Although most people are broken in spirit and just follow the orders shouted at them to get into the trucks, some try to run and many are hiding. Our orders are to shoot anyone trying to escape.

One of my fellow soldiers says, "Just throw a grenade into the building if you think there are people hiding there. It's easier."

I want to stop him but can't.

I feel sick and want to run away myself.

I have to repeat Oma's words in my mind: *Don't stand out. Keep a low profile. Play along.*

I run around and look like I'm chasing someone, but it's just for show.

I shoot high and don't hurt anyone, but I don't help anyone either, so there's nothing to help my conscience.

I feel alone in the crowd.

Chapter 47

I am permitted to write letters to Oma, but they are censored and we can't say anything about our location, how the war is going, or anything that we have done. Basically, there is nothing I can say to her except that I am alive and miss her.

Our commander calls us to a meeting emphasizing the importance of secrecy.

He tells us that an important aircraft factory in Germany was bombed, even though the location was hidden. Apparently, the local newspaper had innocently reported, in its society pages, the names of some top-ranking officials attending parties in this small, obscure town, and that was enough of a clue for the Allies to figure out that there was something there.

Chapter 48

I have no friends in this army.

I keep to myself.

It would be easy for someone close to see that I don't fit in.

I eat whatever food is provided. Admitting to being a vegetarian would be seen as a sign of weakness in my present company. There are so many things I am doing out of character that what I eat just falls into that category.

At the end of the day, I want to make sure that I don't forget who I am, so I picture myself riding through the woods or sitting by the fire with Oma—or anything that is beautiful and serene. I try not to let the ugliness of the war sink in.

Without realizing it, Oma has trained me to survive the day-to-day of the army. With the work that I did around the farm, I have no problem carrying the heavy backpack required of me. Being trained to keep my room and myself tidy from a young age, it is second nature for me to appear in top shape.

My commander, a man whose natural position is upright and who always looks like his uniform has just been pressed, calls me over. He has noticed how my uniform is always clean and crisp and my boots shining. I think this is the reason I am invited to be a guard for him at a dinner party given by his friend's girlfriend.

We hear that her mother worked as a cook in Germany before coming back to Poland and knows how to make all the best dishes. For once, there is something that I am looking forward to, and I make sure to thank the commander.

The home is modest, but we enjoy the food immensely.

It reminds us of our homeland.

We sing songs, and by the warmth of the fire, it almost feels like we are back in Germany.

Franciszka, the old lady hosting the dinner, looks nothing like my tall *oma*, but how she treats me reminds me of home. She tells me to "eat, eat," but she doesn't need to because we are eating with abandonment. Foot soldiers don't get the best food, and tonight is a feast.

After that night, I go back to visit with Franciszka and to have her delicious sauerkraut as often as I can. She tells me that I remind her of her son, Damian.

It's funny how you can find a kindred spirit in the most unlikely of places.

Chapter 49

I don't know what makes me decide to trust her, but I do, in spite of Oma's words.

"Franciszka, you can't believe what we did in the ghetto," and I proceed to tell her everything.

It feels like the burden is lighter to be able to share it.

Despite hearing what we did, she tells me that she knows that I am a good person.

It is what Oma would have said.

I tell her about Oma and how I am all she has. "We're going to be sent into Russia, and I don't think I'll survive that," I say sadly.

SHORTLY AFTERWARD, the commander tells us that half the platoon will move in the next few days.

I know what I have to do.

I sneak out and make my way to Franciszka's house.

Although it is very late at night, she is not asleep and answers the door quickly when she hears my voice.

She puts a finger to her lips to instruct me to whisper. I understand and quietly beg her to help me. "Please, Franciszka, can I hide here?" I try not to sound too anxious, but she knows that I am.

She says nothing but moves to lock the door.

Then she gives me a warm hug while saying in a soft voice, "I will help you."

I think she already knew that I was going to ask her.

I am relieved, but then she says, "There's not much room in this house. The only place that I can hide you is in the attic. Vilheim, it is a very, very small space. I'll show you."

She brings out a ladder from behind some clothes in a closet and motions for me to climb up to the trapdoor that leads to the attic. I look in, and she is right—it's tight up there. The space is no bigger than three feet in height, four feet in width, and ten feet in length.

I will have to lie flat to fit.

Even with this, I am excited at the chance to evade the war.

"Franciszka, thank you, thank you for helping me." I don't know what else to say, but she knows the words come from my heart.

I climb up the ladder to what will be my home for the indefinite future.

Chapter 50

To stay healthy, I do stretches while I am lying flat.

I also figure out a way to do partial sit-ups and push-ups.

When the war is over, I want to be in decent shape.

What I miss the most is walking and moving in general. I think this is how a caged animal must feel. One thing I can do is roll back and forth, if I am careful to do it quietly.

It's a big risk to take to come down from the attic, so I do it quickly and always late at night. I only come down if Franciszka taps our code on the ceiling.

Being caught as a traitor means death by firing squad, not to mention what they would do to Franciszka and her daughter. That keeps my mind and my feet firmly planted in the attic.

There are cracks in the wall that let in some light, and I

welcome that. These cracks, in the winter, are also the same ones that let in the cold air. Sometimes it's so cold that I spend the entire day just shivering. On those days, I imagine how much colder it would have been in Russia.

Franciszka knows that I am a vegetarian, and she is sweet to make those special dishes for me in the middle of a war. Not too often as to attract attention, though. The secret to surviving is to go unnoticed.

Chapter 51

The commander is furious that I am missing and starts a wide search, starting in the forest.

It never occurs to him that a local would hide a German soldier, when Germans took their country away from them.

Late one night, Franciszka taps on the ceiling three times and I go down. "Vilheim, we need to make you dead so they'll stop looking for you."

I say, "How, without my actually dying?"

"Take off your uniform," she says while handing me her son's old clothes.

Then she takes a knife from the kitchen and puts a hole through my shirt. After that, she uses the same knife on one of her chickens and sprinkles the blood on my uniform.

That night, she takes my clothes down to the river and throws them in.

When my clothes are found, everyone blames the Russians and stops looking for me.

I know that the army will contact Oma with the news, and I know that it will be devastating for her, but there is no way of telling her the truth.

I keep myself positive by thinking about how happy she will be when I return after the war.

FRANCISZKA CONTINUES to invite the commander over for dinner, while I am hiding in the attic.

I can't wait to tell my *oma* about this brave woman.

I always thought that courageous people were those who were not afraid. Meeting Franciszka and her daughter, I realize that courageous people are afraid like everyone else. They just act despite the fear.

One day when I go down for a quick break, I see that Franciszka has been crying for a while. She tells me that Damian was killed.

I never knew him, but I feel sad for her. It doesn't seem fair that this should happen to such a good person, and I think that this is how Oma will feel if I don't make it home.

Final Part

HELENA

Chapter 52

The war is intensifying.

One day I come home to find tanks parked right in front of our house. We live close to the river, so it is a strategic position for the Germans.

The tanks are brutal and have crushed everything in their path.

Fresh apples are pressed into the dirt with tread marks.

I am upset that branches of the apple tree were broken off while the tanks maneuvered into position, but my mother reassures me that they will grow back.

"If the roots are crushed, the tree won't survive," I say tearfully.

There is no way of knowing, except with time.

Chapter 53

With so many Germans wandering on the property, our families in hiding are at risk.

After much thought, my mother goes to speak to the officer in charge.

"You know," she says, "my house is very poorly constructed. If you ever had to fire a shot from one of your tanks, it would collapse and bury your soldiers. I would hate to see that happen."

The officer must have thought seriously about what she said because the following week he moves his tanks to another location.

"Always point out what is in the best interest of the other person if you want them to do something. Works on everyone," she says.

Our house, a bunch of wooden boards held together by

nails and plaster, painted white to hide the crooked construction, actually saves us.

Truthfully, most of the homes around us are similarly constructed.

It is the cleverness of my mother that makes the Germans see our house differently from the others.

Chapter 54

The landscape is grim with gray skies and trees that look like they will never be green again.

Some of the buildings in town have been bombed and, with greater priorities elsewhere, they are left in this state of disrepair. There are pieces of broken glass, rubble, and brick in small piles along the sides of the streets. Any wood is quickly taken away for firewood. The beauty of the willow trees by the river is in sharp contrast to the tanks dotted in between. The land beneath our feet—cold, hard, and dry—reflects the suffering that is going on above it.

Food becomes more expensive each day. We would not have been able to feed everyone without Dr. Wolenski's savings and Casmir's generosity. Our neighbors are jealous that we have food, but they don't cause trouble because they think we are connected to the commander.

My mother doesn't play chess, but if she did, it would be with many moves ahead.

THE GERMANS HAVE MOVED more soldiers across the river, and the fighting escalates. When Casmir becomes worried for our safety, I know the situation is deteriorating rapidly.

He is careful with the choice of words in his letters, but I know the underlying message.

"Helena, we no longer need you at the factory. Your employment with us is terminated immediately" really means that he thinks the factory might be bombed at any time.

Chapter 55

You never get used to the fear. It appears out of nowhere, while you are walking, eating, sleeping, and yet you go on because there is nothing else to do. Almost everyone has a family member or friend who has been killed because of the war.

Dr. Wolenski and his family are anxious to hear any news that we have.

We have a code to let Dr. Wolenski know it's safe to come out. It has to be very precise, as walking on the floor can be mistaken for a code. We decide on four quick, successive taps on the floor followed by two slow and then two fast again. The odds of such a combination from walking are slim.

We make sure that Vilheim and Dr. Wolenski never meet.

My mother thinks that it is best that only we know. "Safer for everyone," she says.

I think that Mikolaj is such a good boy. How hard it must be not to be able to run or play for an eight-year-old. I can see how close he is to his mother because when they come up for a quick break in the middle of the night, he never lets go of her hand. Dr. Wolenski keeps track of when it is night and day by his watch. It is dark for them all the time, so there is no way of knowing otherwise.

They develop a system where Felicia and Mikolaj sleep during the day, when the possibility of an unexpected visit is greatest. They are up at night, when it is safer. Dr. Wolenski sleeps at night, but he snores, so Felicia needs to wake him when this happens. As a precaution, they never sleep at the same time.

Bronek doesn't know about Dr. Wolenski or Vilheim either. They never leave the shed because it is too dangerous. I don't know how a large man like Bronek manages to stay cramped up in the loft. It makes me marvel at our will to survive.

I give them a chess set and Bronek spends hours playing with his son. It is too bad that Walter and Mikolaj can't play together. I think they could have been good friends.

Walter, like Mikolaj, is a very good boy. He keeps quiet and learns to speak mostly by hand and facial expressions. Bronek amuses him by doing shadow puppets against the wall.

They have become so good that they can do entire stories that way.

There is a window in the loft with a curtain to prevent people from looking in. From behind the curtain, the family can peek out occasionally.

I know that Bronek has a rotating system, so that they take turns in terms of who can sit by the window each day. It is a small thing for each of them to look forward to.

They can see the apple tree from their window, and when it is in season, I make a point of picking a few each day to leave for them in the loft.

The raid on the ghetto means that as far as we know, all the Jews in Sokal—except for the ones we are hiding—are gone.

I wonder if there are other people like my mother and me who are hiding Jewish families, but there is no way of knowing.

By the beginning of 1944, we have been able to keep this secret for over a year, but all of us are feeling like it will never end.

My mother begins to think that we may be caught, but neither one of us can bring ourselves to make everyone leave.

Chapter 56

It is exhausting to live with constant fear, tempered by nothing but hope.

My mother says to me, "It's hardest on Vilheim because he is hiding alone."

Shortly after a year has passed, we notice that Vilheim has not come down for several days. My mother has difficulty climbing the ladder, so she asks me to go up to the attic to check on him.

I see that the food we left him has remained untouched. He is lying so still that I panic and think he's dead! Then he opens his eyes, but there is no life in them. It's awkward, but I manage to crouch down to lift up his head and give him some water. It rolls down the side of his mouth since he makes no effort to swallow. Not knowing what to do, I come back down and tell my mother what has happened.

"What should we do?" I ask.

She responds with a question. "Does he have a fever?"

"No, I don't think so. He didn't feel warm to me when I lifted his head," I reply.

"I see," my mother says.

"Should we let Dr. Wolenski know about Vilheim and see if he can help?" I ask.

Surprisingly, my mother says, "No, that won't help."

I think she has given up on Vilheim, but I should have known better with my mother.

"His problem can't be solved by medicine," she says. "I need to talk to him."

So even though it is painful for her, she climbs up the ladder.

I follow after her to hear what she is saying to him.

She says, "Vilheim, do you want your life to end here? What about your *oma*? What about your farm? Don't you want to ride that horse of yours? I don't know how to ride a horse, but it must be a wonderful feeling. You will have that life again, but not if you die here."

Her remedy is a heavy dose of optimism blended with some truth.

She says, "Don't give up now, Vilheim, when we are so close. There is news that Hitler will lose at any moment.

We're almost there. Just a little longer and you will be back on your farm. If you quit, who will look after your *oma* and all the animals on your farm?"

My mother uses everything.

Each day she goes up there with this message. She brings him food and water and makes sure that he gets it down.

Within two weeks, Vilheim is back to the way he was.

My mother and I don't want him to take a step backward, so we keep him posted with news that my mother makes up about how the Germans are losing badly here and there.

Not knowing much about geography, we name places from an atlas that Dr. Wolenski brought for Mikolaj.

Miraculously, the news that my mother is making up begins to come true.

Hope is a strategy after all.

Chapter 57

Although extremely dangerous, Casmir makes the trip to see me.

When I see his face at my door, the face that I see every time I close my eyes, I can hardly believe it.

I run to him, laughing and crying at the same time.

Feeling delirious with joy and relieved that he is safe, I wrap my arms around his waist, not wanting to let go.

He gently lifts my face with both hands and looks at me. “Where is that wonderful smile I saw the first time I met you?”

I love his voice and how it makes everything sound magical.

Chapter 58

When I was young, I asked my mother, "How will I know if I'm in love?"

Her answer was, "You will know."

Thinking that her response was vague and wanting more, I persisted.

"No, really, tell me how I will know."

She said, "There is nothing more to say except that if you don't know, then you're not in love."

Now I know exactly what she means.

I love this man with my entire being.

When I am with him, the war is pushed away. There is kindness, beauty, and hope.

He is my refuge, and my life.

No one melts me like he does. No one is him for me.

Chapter 59

In the privacy of our house, Casmir secretly confides that he is hearing that the war is not going well for the Germans. He says, "Hitler made a mistake breaking with Stalin, and with the Americans now in the war too, the tide is turning on Germany."

I can hardly wait to hear more.

He says, "Hitler is stubborn and even when it doesn't look like he can win, he keeps fighting."

Casmir continues. "They are so short of soldiers that they are now recruiting sixteen-year-olds and old men in Germany. I am kept out of the army only because our factory makes uniforms for them."

This development is so exciting that we share it with Bronek, Dr. Wolenski, and Vilheim as soon as it is safe to do so.

If they could have shouted with joy, they would have.

With this new optimism, all of us know that we just need to hang on for a little longer, and it becomes more bearable.

CASMIR CANNOT STAY LONG.

He comes to the house with crates full of cooking oil, flour, salt, and potatoes to say good-bye.

It is his way of loving me.

Before he leaves, he holds me so close that I can feel his heartbeat.

He bends down to kiss me, and I taste the salt of his tears on my lips.

It is a taste that stays with me long after he is gone.

Chapter 60

Soon after Casmir leaves, the tide turns with the Russians crossing the Bug River and the Germans now in retreat.

I can't believe it.

Although the war is not yet over, the Germans leave Sokal.

My mother and I look at each other in disbelief. Can it really be? We have waited and hoped for this moment for so long that it takes awhile for our minds and bodies to absorb the news.

We have saved both families and a German soldier.

We have all endured.

ON JULY 19, 1944, we move the kitchen table and help Dr. Wolenski, Felicia, and Mikolaj out of their hiding place. They squint as they come out into the light, but they are smiling.

We also tell Bronek and his family that it is safe to come down from the loft. They come down the ladder slowly with bodies stiff from being cramped for so long. They are hugging and crying, as are all of us by now.

My mother taps on the ceiling three times and opens the trapdoor to shout, "The soldiers are gone!"

Vilheim comes down from the attic with a big bump on his forehead.

He was so excited by the news that he sat up without thinking and hit his head.

My mother is careful to keep him hidden in the house, as he would surely be shot by the Russians.

We don't tell our neighbors that we have hidden Jews because there still lingers anti-Semitic sentiment.

In our small house, it is the first time that Bronek and Dr. Wolenski meet. They can't believe that Franciszka has hidden both their families.

Dr. Wolenski is astonished because he knows Anelie, having delivered Walter.

Anelie turns to Bronek with tears in her eyes and says, "Our baby."

Bronek replies in a soft voice, "There's nothing we could have done," and holds Anelie, who is now sobbing. He tries to comfort her with, "We'll always remember her."

The boys look at each other curiously, but they soon act like they have always known each other. Kids make friends so easily.

When Bronek sees Vilheim, he is angry at first. Then he remembers the night with the German soldier who turned the other way.

"I saw you sliding under the barbed wire," Vilheim says, "but I didn't shoot you."

Chapter 61

To be safe, everyone stays with us until it is clear that Germany has lost the war. Then my mother asks Bronek for a favor. "I helped you; now it's your turn to help someone else. Let Vilheim travel with you out of Poland. Say he is your brother. He can make his way back to Germany on his own after that."

How can we do this? Help a German soldier? But then Bronek thinks of that night and also this: a request from Franciszka—how can he refuse?

And that is how a Jewish family, hiding a German soldier, leaves Poland.

Vilheim leaves wearing Damian's clothes, and I feel that, in some way, my brother would have been proud of us.

Bronek, Anelie, Walter, and Bryda immigrate to the

United States. There, they make their way to Texas, where Bronek works on a ranch, just as he did before the war.

Dr. Wolenski, Felicia, and Mikolaj move to Palestine, where they need doctors.

Vilheim returns to the farm, where his *oma* embraces him with tears of joy.

She can't believe her eyes when she sees him and thanks God for answering her prayers.

We all find our own place in the world, but all of us are forever connected by a bond that will survive time and distance.

Chapter 62

My mother and I move to Switzerland, where Casmir now lives.

In a country as untouched by the war as any could possibly be in Europe, he asks me to marry him.

I say what he must already know: "I have always wanted to be with you."

He says, "But you couldn't because your mother was hiding Jews."

I look at him incredulously. "You knew? How?"

He answers, "Nobody eats that much food, Helena."

"Why didn't you say something then?" I ask.

Without malice, he replies, "I thought you would tell me when you were ready."

"We didn't want to put your life in danger." These words sound weak but are the truth.

"I understand," he says. "Just promise me one thing: no more secrets when we're married."

I smile and say, "None, I promise."

Chapter 63

On my wedding day, my mother is helping me with my dress when she asks, "Do you know when a woman is the most beautiful?"

I answer, "When she is loved."

She says, "That's exactly right," and so I know she is happy for Casmir and me.

Chapter 64

Dr. Wolenski never forgets my mother and sends her money every year.

Bronek sends us endless parcels from the United States, and my daughter wonders how it is that we get presents from people all over the world.

I tell her that her grandmother Franciszka, for whom she is named, is an angel that had so much love to give that it spread around the world. "All that love is just coming back," I say.

Love is the only thing that you get more of when you give it away.

Chapter 65

My mother is the most incredible woman that I know.

She is softhearted yet strong willed.

She is compassionate yet unwavering in principle.

She is a loving mother, yet she risked my life to save others.

She lost her son in the conflict between the Jews and Germans, yet she held no bitterness toward either one.

She hid two Jewish families and a German soldier for twenty months and asked for nothing in return.

Chapter 66

After my mother passed away, some people asked me, "Why? Why do you think she hid the Jews?"

The honest answer is, I don't know.

We didn't think about our motives, my mother and I.

There was certainly nothing to be gained by our actions at the time.

We weren't religious, and we didn't have an affinity with the Jewish people.

I think it simply came down to not being able to turn away people who would have otherwise faced a certain death.

Does that make us exceptional? Or is it only exceptional because so many others chose not to do the same thing?

The standard defines the exception.

We did not think of ourselves as extraordinary.

All we knew was that we needed to be strong to see it through, and thankfully we did.

Chapter 67

I miss my mother.

When I see her in my mind, I see this tobacco-chewing, defiant, small woman with a spirit that would not be dominated. She always wore the same skirt that looked too big for her, and it never occurred to me until many years later that she might have liked a new dress for herself. I was too self-absorbed to realize this at the time.

IN FRONT OF where we live now, I have planted an apple tree with seeds we kept from the tree that Damian planted.

An apple tree is again the first thing I see in the morning from my bedroom window.

I am grateful, and it is a peaceful feeling.

Regret for the things we did can be tempered by time;

it is regret for the things we did not do that is inconsolable.

—Sydney J. Harris

Epilogue

This book is fictional, but it was inspired by the true story of Franciszka Halamajowa, who with her daughter saved the lives of fifteen Jews in Poland during the Second World War. She also hid a young German soldier in her attic at the same time. Her son died while transporting a wagon full of supplies to partisan Jews hiding in the forest.

Before the war, there were six thousand Jews in Sokal, Poland. Only thirty survived the war and half of those because of one Polish woman, Franciszka.

I believe that all of us, like Franciszka, have within us the potential to be great. Sometimes we coast through life without this potential surfacing because life has been easy on us.

When we have much to lose, but still choose to do the right thing, we uncover the nobility that is within all of us. To endure what is unbearable and to do it with grace, that is how we know that we have arrived.

Trip to Israel

In 2012, I visited Yad Vashem, the Holocaust museum in Jerusalem, where there is a tree planted and a plaque to honor Franciszka Halamajowa and her daughter, Helena.

People who were not Jewish, but who nevertheless risked their lives to help the Jews escape execution during the Holocaust, are recognized as "the Righteous among the Nations" in Israel. This is how Franciszka and her daughter are remembered.

It was my son, Matthew, who actually found the tree, as

bushes had grown in front of the plaque, preventing me from seeing it initially.

Upon seeing their names there in print before me, I was overcome with emotion.

I had written about this woman and her daughter and I had imagined their lives, but here was evidence that they indeed did exist. I didn't realize how deeply I would feel until this moment.

Planting a tree to remember them by feels so right.

Acknowledgments

I am nothing but truthful when I say that this book would not have been possible without the incredible generosity of time and insight provided to me by some very special friends.

Brian Goldstein read the initial draft of the story when it was only about ten pages long and provided me with an enthusiastic response that encouraged me to proceed further.

From there, I ventured to have Richard Self read it, who told me that he could see exactly what was happening through my words and that the story had an inspirational feel to it like the classic *Jonathan Livingston Seagull.* Well, that provided me with quite the lift. His fourteen-year-old daughter, Jacqueline, read it and liked it too, so now I had some confidence about the range and reach of the story.

I was fortunate to then have Jack Gluckman leave me a voice mail saying that he had just read the book and to give him a call immediately. He said, "Honestly, when you asked me to read your book, I thought, okay, I'll read a few pages to be polite, but you're not a writer, so how good could it be? You know, I couldn't put it down and read it all in one go with tears in my eyes when I finished. Thank you for sharing it with me." It just doesn't get much better than that.

He then asked me if it would be all right to pass it on to friends of his who were from the publishing industry. You guessed it; my answer was "Absolutely."

One veteran of the industry said it was too short and was not interested in proceeding further. Howard Wells, however, a twenty-year veteran of the industry who is now retired, said to me, "This is authentic and reads like poetry." For Howard those words are as good as it gets.

"Not too short?" I asked.

He said, "Have you read *The Little Prince*?"

Okay, that's about as short a book as you can get, and yes, I have read and loved it! It works on so many levels.

Howard followed up with, "I read more books in a month than most people read in a year, so trust me when I say I like it."

Hey, who wants to argue with that?

The lesson I have learned is that a positive response cannot only motivate but lead to even greater achievement than initially thought possible. I sharpened my iPad and kept going.

Elayne Freeman, a librarian with a special interest in Holocaust literature for young adults, read the book in fine detail. Being an expert on both the Holocaust and of that time period, she was able to provide me with specific suggestions to make it more credible. I welcomed every word and proceeded to rewrite.

Next, I dropped off a copy for Arnold Noyek, who is a creative thinker, a leading educator, and an innovator in global health. He is greatly admired for his vision and his peace initiatives in the Middle East. I couldn't believe his response. He read it that night and called me right away. I could feel his energy bouncing off the walls.

Now Arnold has more energy than just about anyone I know, but he says things like, "Jen, this is brilliant and I see great possibilities for this book to promote peace and understanding."

He also sends me an e-mail: "This manuscript has great adaptability as a curriculum tool for teaching ethics, values, and the ultimate commitment to living a life where human concerns for engaging in tolerance, kindness, and doing the right thing trumps all."

Wow, do these words turn me on or what? Arnold makes

me want to make the book even better, and so I pursue more research and fill in details on dates and time lines that give the story more authenticity.

About now, I remember that Lori Lothian is a law professor and a great editor, so I call and ask if she will have a look. She graciously reads the book not once but multiple times and suggests that I pay attention to providing subtle details that add realism to the story. Her suggestions make the story come together like a well-planned meal where not only is the food pleasing, but the dishes and napkins all match too.

Every time I think the story has reached its destination and cannot possibly be improved, fate sends me someone to take it one level higher. At times, it feels that there is a greater force at work.

Lori has two nephews—Owen, twelve, and Branton, fifteen—who read it and love it too. Owen says it's going to be a *New York Times* bestseller and then runs out of the car to knock on a tree (wood). This story makes me laugh and endears me to these boys, whom I have met only once.

By now, I am thinking the book is pretty much finished. Sitting at my desk and reflecting on what a journey it has all been, I see it—a quote that is typed out and sitting upright in a plastic stand that a friend of mine, Tony Hamblin, gave me years ago as a reminder of how I should live my life. It talks about how our biggest regrets are not what we did, but what we did not do. It was so perfect for where I was at that moment, and also what the story is about. That is why I decided to end the story with this quote.

After the manuscript was completed, I asked some other people to read it. Their responses, touching and inspirational, were humbling. You can see their words at the beginning of the book.

Finally, the passage from manuscript to book was only possible with the wisdom and advice of a wonderful man . . . Alan Bower, and the team at iUniverse.

Thank you for letting me share this voyage with you. It was filled with the kindness of so many.

Living with gratitude,
J. L. Witterick